MY STORYBOOK OF
FAIRIES & ELVES

MY STORYBOOK OF
FAIRIES & ELVES

A COLLECTION OF 20 MAGICAL STORIES

WRITTEN BY NICOLA BAXTER
ILLUSTRATED BY BEVERLIE MANSON

H
HERMES
HOUSE

This edition is published by Hermes House, an imprint of Anness Publishing Ltd,
108 Great Russell Street, London WC1B 3NA; info@anness.com

www.hermeshouse.com; www.annesspublishing.com

If you like the images in this book and would like to investigate using them for publishing, promotions
or advertising, please visit our website www.practicalpictures.com for more information.

A CIP catalogue record for this book is available from the British Library.

Publisher: Joanna Lorenz
Editors: Sally Delaney and Elizabeth Young
Designer: Amanda Hawkes
Cover Designer: Elizabeth Young
Production Designer: Amy Barton
Illustrator: Beverlie Manson/Advocate
Production Controller: Pirong Wang

PUBLISHER'S NOTE
The author and publishers have made every effort to ensure that this book is safe for its intended use,
and cannot accept any legal responsibility or liability for any harm or injury arising from misuse.

Manufacturer: Anness Publishing Ltd, 108 Great Russell Street, London WC1B 3NA, England
For Product Tracking go to: www.annesspublishing.com/tracking
Batch: 6060-23386-0004

CONTENTS

THE MAGICAL WORLD OF FAIRIES & ELVES 8

THE *DREAMLAND* *FAIRIES* 86

THE FAIRY PRINCESSES 164

THE MAGICAL WORLD OF FAIRIES & ELVES

The Time
of
Beginnings

When the first tiny green shoots appear above the velvety earth, it is still very cold. Sparkling frost often glitters on cobwebs stretched between dead grasses at the edge of the forest. But those green shoots mean something, and the fairies know it. Although it is not warm enough for their wings to work, and they stay huddled in the sheltered places where they have spent the winter, they know that spring is on its way. And each time that the sun shines palely down, more tiny tendrils push towards the light.

Day by day, the sun becomes warmer. Fairies peep out of their homes and turn their faces to its golden glow. The green shoots have grown, and little buds appear. One day a fairy finds the first snowdrop nodding gently in the breeze and runs to tell her friends.

"Soon she will be here!" she cries. As all fairies know, when the very first flowers of spring appear, the Queen of the Fairies flies around her realm to greet her little people and tell them that the Time of Beginnings has come.

The Queen's first visit this year is to a clearing near the edge of an ancient forest. It is one of the places she loves best. As she looks up at the noble old trees, she remembers that fairies are older still, and their magic goes back to the beginning of everything.

Then the Queen raises her hand, and a tiny fairy plays a silvery tune on a little flute made of reed. At once, all the fairies who live nearby come hurrying to the clearing. They clap their hands with pleasure at the sight of their much-loved leader, and curtsey or bow as they approach her.

"Now, my fairies," says the Queen. "We have all rested during the cold days of winter, but our rest is over. The Time of Beginnings is here, and we must be busy.
What news do you have for me?"

The fairies tell her about all the little signs they have seen. They mention the birds with wisps of straw in their mouths, looking for somewhere to build a nest. They tell of the squirrels, mending their untidy drays ready to raise another family. They describe the lively mice and voles, running in and out of holes in the riverbank, getting ready for the new families they will have in a few weeks' time.

"Then you know what to do," says the Queen. "Are you in charge, as usual, Vernal? I will be back when the spring is at its height. Good luck!"

The fairies do know what to do. It is their job to help all the baby creatures come safely into the world. Of course, the babies' mothers and fathers do that, too, but fairies can help in unexpected ways. From dusk until dawn, Vernal sits at the foot of a great oak tree and advises the fairies who bring her news of problems in the wide world.

"There is a little fluffy duckling stuck in the mud at the edge of the lake," reports an anxious little fairy.

"Don't worry," says Vernal. "It happens every year. Her mother will soon pull her out. Grown-up ducks know all about mud!"

"There is a nest in the hawthorn tree with four beautiful eggs in it," cries a little fairy called Cobweb, "and I haven't seen the parent birds since last night."

"That is a long time," says Vernal. "Find feathers and thistledown to keep those eggs warm until the parents return."

"The wild daffodils at the edge of the wood seem to have no flowers this year," explains Bumble, scurrying into the clearing. "What can we do?"

Vernal sighs. "Sometimes that happens," she says. "Under the ground the flowers for next year are already beginning to form. We just have to be patient."

Then, one morning, Vernal comes out into the wood and feels warm sunlight on her face. She smiles with delight. The little flute summons all the nearby fairies together again.

"My dears," calls Vernal, raising her voice to be heard, "this morning when I came outside, the sun warmed my face and I knew that it was time. You may fly!"

At once there is chattering and laughing from the fairies. It is one of the most exciting days of the year. In the winter, it is too cold for fairies to stretch their wings and fly. They need to open them in the sunshine so that they become bright and strong. Today the air will once again be filled with fairies.

"I'm glad," says Cobweb. "I've been climbing up to check on that birds' nest every day this week. It will be so much easier to fly."

Slowly, the fairies shake out their wings and let the sunshine smooth out the crinkles. Then with a little humming sound, they rise into the air, giggling with pleasure. They wave their arms in the warm breeze and twirl and point their toes. One or two of the little ones try advanced acrobatics and land with a bump on the grassy ground below.

"Come on!" laughs Vernal. "There's still work to do!"

From that day, spring cannot happen fast enough. Leaves rush to unfurl in the forest. Flowers flood the valleys.

And in the nests and tiny homes nearby, little squeaking voices are heard as the first babies join the wakening world.

"Don't fairies have babies?" asks Violet, a tiny fairy who has brought a beautiful, broken eggshell to show Vernal.

"Well, fairies live for ever, it seems," says Vernal, "so we don't need to have babies to take over from us. But sometimes, when it feels as if spring is at its height, and the whole world is busy and full of beginnings, a sparkling dewdrop suddenly becomes too beautiful to bear, and a new little fairy appears. That's what happened last year when *you* appeared!"

For the next few days, each time she passes a cobweb glittering with dew, or sees shining drops on a twig or branch, Violet stops and waits, holding her breath. Nothing happens.

Then, early one morning, Violet flies by a wild cherry tree and gasps at the beautiful sight. It has been lightly raining, and little crystal drops still hang among the pale pink flowers. Violet lands gently on a branch to look more closely, and just at that moment, right next to her, the sunlight catches a raindrop and makes it sparkle. With a little silvery sound it vanishes, leaving a tiny, smiling fairy, new to the world.

The Royal
Flying Race

All through the spring, fairies flit and fairies fly, checking on baby birds, sprinkling raindrops on tiny plants, and clearing away dead leaves so that the sunshine can reach the shy little flowers peeping out beneath trees and hedges. Each day, the weather becomes a little warmer, and all around, the whole world is bursting into life.

One morning, two little fairies meet on a branch high in a noble tree.

"Look out!" calls Bramble. "I'm coming in to land!"

He whizzes down and settles on the branch where a pretty little fairy called Leafe is already sitting.

"Hey, that was good!" laughs Leafe. "Your flying has really improved. Some of us still haven't recovered from the time you bumped into us over the bean field, and we all landed on that manure heap! We were smelly for weeks!"

"I was very young then," says Bramble with dignity. "You can't expect expert flying from a baby. But I've been practising. Look!"

He bounces off the branch and does a full twizzle with wing twist.

"Ah, but can you do this?" asks Leafe, elegantly swooping through the air in a figure-of-eight pattern and performing a complicated one-leg landing.

The two fairies try to outdo each other for the rest of the morning, trying acrobatics and chasing through the leaves, but it is only when they are sitting breathless on the branch again that Bramble has an idea.

"We could have a race!" he cries.

"I'm exhausted," replies Leafe, "I couldn't possibly race you now."

"I don't mean me," says Bramble impatiently. "And I don't mean now."

"Then what in Fairyland are you talking about?" asks Leafe.

Bramble explains that he is thinking of a race for all the fairies. It will take their minds off all the hard work they have been doing recently and be a fun event for everyone.

"It's not a bad idea," Leafe admits, "but it wouldn't be fair, really, would it, if older fairies raced against little ones? And some fairies are, well, *rounder* than others."

"We could have different races for different ages and sizes," says Bramble. "Then it would be fair. Or, the better fliers could start after the little ones, so we all flew in the same race but started at different times."

"That is quite a good idea," Leafe agrees. "Let's tell the others."

Before long, news of the flying race has fluttered around Fairyland. Most fairies think it will be fun. Even the Queen hears of it and, although she doesn't think she will have time to compete herself, she agrees to give the prizes at the end.

"That makes it a *royal* flying race," says Leafe proudly.
On the afternoon agreed, dozens of fairies meet in the clearing in the forest. Not all of them want to race. Some have come to cheer on their friends or watch the presentation at the end.
It is all very well organized. The course is around the edge of the forest and back into the glade. The first fairy to touch the trunk of the old oak tree will be the winner, but there will be prizes for runners-up, too.

First, the smallest, youngest fairies line up. "Get ready, flutter and FLY!" cries Azure, who has been appointed Race-Starter.

The little fairies flit off. After five minutes, measured on a dandelion clock, of course, the slightly older fairies also line up.

"Get ready, flutter and FLY!" They're off!

Last of all, the really experienced, fast-flying fairies get ready to set off. They bounce eagerly on their toes, and there are a few false starts before they are finally away.

"They'll catch the little ones easily," says Azure, watching the best fliers disappear.

"I'm not so sure," says a musical voice. The Fairy Queen has arrived. "One or two of those baby fliers are showing real promise. There's a tiny fairy called Primrose who has the speediest little wings I've ever seen."

"True, Your Highness," says Azure, bowing low, "but Swift is a very fast flier and knows how to skim through the wind."

The Queen looks up. "Yes, I hadn't noticed that the wind has grown stronger. I do hope all the fairies come back safely." The leaves above begin to rustle more and more, and even quite large branches begin to move.

At last, however, the fairies begin to return. First back is an experienced flier called Barley. It is a while before she can catch her breath. "Swift was ahead of me," she gasps at last, "but little Primrose was even ahead of him. Then, a huge gust of wind swept the tiny fairy up towards the clouds. Swift flew after her, but I haven't seen them since."

One by one, the flying fairies return – all except Swift and Primrose. The Queen looks grave, until a sudden squeal above her makes everyone look up. There is Swift, with Primrose in his arms.

Well, Barley won the race, of course, but everyone agrees that the real winners are the fairies who arrived last of all.

"Swift and Primrose are without doubt our finest fliers," says the Queen, presenting them with crowns of petals and dewdrops. Everyone cheers. "Hip, hip, hooray for Swift, who flies faster than the wind, and for Primrose, who flies faster still!"

The Butterfly Babies

Fairies are busy in the spring, but as the days lengthen and become warmer, they become even busier. There are simply so many flowers to flit among, checking that the bees are doing their work properly, and more baby creatures are born every day. Looking after little ones is a job that fairies take very seriously. Well, I suppose, they are little themselves. But even fairies sometimes make mistakes …

Young Catkin and his friend Rosebud are very active little fairies. They can't wait to do all the jobs that big fairies do. Sometimes that means they don't listen as carefully as they should to what older fairies say.

Each evening during the spring and summer, as the sun begins to set over the fields and woodland, little groups of fairies gather together so that the more experienced ones can tell youngsters all the important things they need to know. How to tell the difference between a robin's egg and a blackbird's egg, for example. How to help a baby rabbit who has fallen into a puddle. How to make sure that birds always leave a few berries on a bush so that new plants can grow for the future.

It is all interesting and useful information, and it is lucky that fairies live such a long, long time, because it takes ages to learn everything there is to know about the world of nature.

Catkin and Rosebud certainly have a lot to learn, so they really shouldn't be chatting and giggling together when Silverbark is giving an important talk about butterflies. They hear the bit about butterflies laying eggs, and they half hear Silverbark's wise words about how to be safe when helping a butterfly who likes to land on nettles, but then they are too busy tickling each other and laughing to hear very much at all.

Hawthorn, the fairy who is speaking, looks severely in the direction of the two naughty little fairies and coughs loudly. Catkin and Rosebud behave for about five minutes and then go back to their giggling. In the end, Hawthorn brings the meeting to a close. "No doubt we have all been working very hard," he says kindly, "and some of us, especially the little ones, are tired. It's hard to learn something new when you are sleepy. Tomorrow I will be talking about snails and slugs, and how to help them."

It's a pity that Catkin and Rosebud don't listen more carefully, because the very next day, as they are flying about at the edge of the wood, they spot a beautiful peacock butterfly, sitting on some young nettles.

The two little fairies settle on a nearby branch and watch carefully. The butterfly lazily spreads her wings in the sunshine. She doesn't seem to be in any trouble or to need any help.

"I wish we could find a really grown-up job to do," whispers Catkin. "I'm tired of other fairies thinking we need to be helped all the time."

"So am I," says Rosebud. "Oh, Catkin, look!"

As the beautiful butterfly flaps her wings and flits away, one of the nettle leaves stirs in the wind and shows that underneath she has laid lots and lots of tiny eggs. The eggs are olive green, so they are quite hard to see on the green nettle leaves.

"This is a job for us!" cries Catkin. "Those eggs are going to hatch into baby butterflies. We must make sure they are safe. I expect baby butterflies are a bit like baby fairies. They probably can't fly very well to start with. We'll need to come here every day to look after them."

Catkin and Rosebud are very excited about their butterfly babies. They agree that they will keep their special job a secret. "Otherwise," says Rosebud, "other fairies will take over, and we won't see *our* butterflies fly away!"

Well, the little fairies keep a careful watch on the eggs. It seems as though nothing happens for ages. After a while, the little fairies become bored and only visit very quickly each day to check what is going on. Gradually, even this seems rather boring. One day, Catkin and Rosebud are so busy chasing ladybirds that they don't bother to visit the butterfly eggs at all.

"I don't believe those eggs are ever going to be butterflies," says Rosebud when she remembers. "We'll go tomorrow, though. We wouldn't want to miss anything."

"Something's been puzzling me," says Catkin slowly. "I mean, how is a big butterfly going to fit into one of those tiny eggs?"

"It won't be big, silly!" laughs Rosebud. "It will be tiny. A baby. Then it will grow big."

Catkin still looks puzzled. He is thinking that he has never actually *seen* a small, baby butterfly. But he doesn't say anything. He doesn't want Rosebud to laugh at him.

The next day, the two little fairies fly back to the edge of the wood and settle down on their branch as usual. They glance at the nettle patch and suddenly freeze with horror. Where there had been hundreds of tiny green eggs, there is suddenly a swarming mass of tiny black wriggling things.

"Yeeeuch!" cries Catkin. "What are those?"

But Rosebud has a worse thought. "Oh dear, oh dear," she sobs, "those horrible black things have eaten all the butterfly eggs!"

It seems this must be true. There are no longer any eggs to be seen.

Catkin and Rosebud feel very guilty. "If only we had come yesterday," sniffs Rosebud, "we might have been able to save them. You know, I think this must often happen. I've never actually seen a tiny baby butterfly."

"That's just what I was thinking," says Catkin. "We'll come back when the black squiggly things have gone. There might still be just a few eggs hiding under the leaves."

But although the fairies come back to look several times, the black squiggly things don't go away. They obviously like nettle leaves very, very much and spend their time happily munching through them. As they munch, they get bigger and bigger.

Rosebud and Catkin don't dare to fly too near to the black things. They stay on their branch and watch. Now they are big, the black things have horrible branching spikes on their backs and little white dots on their squiggly bodies.

"I've got another worry," says Catkin one day. He has a lot of worries at the moment, most of them caused because he doesn't really understand what is happening. "Those black things are getting bigger every day. What if they … just keep on growing?"

Rosebud nearly falls off her branch, the idea is so frightening. What if the black monsters grow as big as a squirrel? As big as a cow? As big as an oak tree?

"And it might be all our fault," she whispers. "Those monsters might eat up the whole world … and we let them do it."

"Perhaps we should tell someone," says Catkin, but Rosebud shakes her head. "They'll be so cross," she says. "Please, please, promise me you'll keep our secret." Catkin promises. *He's* worried that the other fairies will be cross, too.

But the squiggly things just keep getting bigger and bigger, until one day, they're not there at all!

"They've escaped!" cries Catkin. "Oh no!"

There are some strange green things hanging from some of the nettles, but the little fairies are too frightened to notice them.

They fly as fast as they can back to their homes and are so bothered that they fly straight into Silverbark among the trees.

"Ouch!" "Ouf!" "Ow!"

The three fairies pick themselves up and brush leaves and twigs from their wings. Silverbark is about to give the little ones a lecture on safe flying, when he sees their worried faces.

"Whatever is the matter?" he asks.

Then the whole story comes tumbling out. Silverbark asks a lot of questions. Were the eggs black or white? How big were the things? He doesn't seem very worried.

"But don't you see," sobs Catkin, "they might eat all of us!"

Silverbark smiles. "Come with me," he says. He flies with the little fairies through the forest and into the fields. He shows them lots and lots of squiggly things. Some are black, some are green, some are yellow. All of them are munching and munching.

"They are called caterpillars," Silverbark explains. "The different kinds all like something different to eat. But they do no harm. In fact, they do something rather wonderful."

"But they ate the butterfly's eggs," says Rosebud. "That's awful."

"They didn't eat the eggs," laughs Silverbark. "They hatched out of them!"

"They can't have done!" Catkin is shocked. "Babies look like their mothers and fathers. Caterpillars don't look at all like beautiful butterflies!"

"That is what is so wonderful," Silverbark smiles. "When a caterpillar has grown very big and fat, it changes itself."

"Into a butterfly?"

"No, into a chrysalis. Those green things you saw where the caterpillars had been were chrysalises. They're like little rooms where a wonderful change takes place. But we have to wait."

It is one sunny morning a few weeks later that Catkin and Rosebud sit with Silverbark on a branch and watch something amazing. The green things are almost transparent now.

You can see parts of patterns inside. And when one of them begins to split open, a wonderful butterfly crawls out.

"But its wings are all crumpled," cries Rosebud.

"It's just like fairies' wings in the winter," whispers Silverbark. "They have to warm in the sun and stretch out. It doesn't take long. Look!"

As he speaks, the butterfly stretches out its wings, flaps them once or twice, and lifts off into the air. The little fairies are so enchanted that they don't giggle or wriggle at all.

Silverbark looks at their shining faces and smiles. They will be good little fairies one day … quite soon.

The Blossom Ball

The warm summer sun climbs daily into the sky, bringing with it the scents and sounds of long, lazy days. Soon there comes a time when each day seems to pass from dusk to dawn without real darkness in between. On the longest day of the whole year, the fairies prepare for their midsummer party. It is called the Blossom Ball.

All fairies love to sing and dance, but the Blossom Ball is special. It is at this party that the little fairies are helped to choose the jobs they will do in the wide world and their final fairy names.

Most little fairies already have a name, of course. It is usually something cuddly and kind that older fairies have chosen for them, such as Bumble or Tinkle. Or it may be based on the way they look. It is not surprising if a pretty little fairy who loves to wear pink is called Rosebud, for example. But at the Blossom Ball, these little fairies have the chance to change or add to their names, and many of them do.

It is a tradition that nothing is done to prepare for the ball until the day itself. There is a good reason for that. Although the ball is usually held on the very longest day of the year, good weather is really important.

If summer showers begin in the morning, the Queen announces that the ball will not be held until fine weather comes again. So it is not until the day itself that the fairies begin to get ready.

First there are garlands to be made. Little fairies are sent off to find flowers, always being careful to leave plenty behind, and older fairies use needles borrowed from friendly pine trees to join them together to make wonderful decorations.

Next the food and drink must be assembled. The fairies go to their stores in the hollows of trees and find the ingredients for honey drink and buttercup bread, cowslip cake and pollen pudding. There is stirring and tasting and laughter.

Last comes the most important part of all. Costumes! This is the fairies' carnival time, and they each try to create the most beautiful dresses and the highest hats. They use petals and feathers, berries and seeds, sewn together with cobweb thread. Some fairies wear glittering dewdrops in their hair. Others wrap themselves in thistledown cloaks.

And then there are the sillier costumes. Fairies compete to wear the highest hat. They walk on twig-stilts and pretend to be spiders. They dress up as butterflies, flowers and fruits. Meanwhile, the musicians practice their pieces. Sometimes a nightingale can be persuaded to sing in the branches above.

Everyone is busy and laughing until the moment comes for the ball to begin. Then, as the fairies all gather, some fluttering into

the air for a better view, the Queen makes her grand entrance. Each year, her own costume is more spectacular than the last. A fairy cheer goes up as she takes her place. The ball begins.

It is in the middle of the party, when fairies have rested from their dancing and refreshed themselves with delicious food and drink, that the Queen claps her hands and announces that the Naming is about to begin.

One by one, the smallest fairies step forward, sometimes with friends when they are too shy to speak for themselves. To each, the Queen kindly asks the same questions. First to stand before her today is Primrose, wearing a lovely dandelion dress of yellow and green.

"Ah," says the Queen, "I know your name already. You are Primrose, the fastest little flier in Fairyland."

Primrose blushes and flutters her wings with excitement.

"I would guess that you would like work that uses your excellent flying skills," says the Queen. "What will it be?"

"Please, I would like to be a weather-watcher," says Primrose.

The watching fairies nod with approval. Weather-watchers fly around all day, looking for the tiny signs that show a change is on the way. Fairies need to know when a storm is brewing, or if the rain that tiny plants need is going to be delayed.

"And your name?" smiles the Queen. "I'm not sure that Primrose is a very good name for a weather-watcher, or for a famous flier."

"I'd like you to choose," whispers the tiny fairy.

"Then I shall call you Skysinger," says the Queen, "because you will bring the songs of the seasons back to us each day."

Skysinger flutters into the air to show how pleased she is, and a little shower of yellow petals floats around her.

Before long all the smallest fairies have come to the Queen. Some decide to keep their old names. Others choose something new. All go away with smiles on their faces.

At last, only one little fairy is left. She is beautiful, and wears a dress of white daisy petals.

"Please, Your Highness," she says, in answer to the Queen's first question, "I don't yet have any name."

"But what do your friends call when they want you to come to them?" asks the Queen, puzzled.

"They don't need to call," says the little fairy. "Somehow I know without them saying anything when they need me, so I am there before they call."

The Queen looks carefully at the fairy. "Is this true?" she asks. Fairies standing nearby nod that it is.

"And what work would you like to do?" asks the Queen.

"I don't know that either," says the little fairy. "You see, everything is so interesting. I want to know about all the things that fairies do. I want to see everything. Don't make me choose!"

The Queen smiles with tears of joy in her eyes. "Well," she says, "I knew this day would come. You have a great, great deal to learn, little one. And I will not be giving you a name today.

But one day, far in the future, when it is time for me to fly towards the sun, you will be called Queen of the Fairies – the most magical name of all."

Now there really is something to celebrate. As the Queen hugs the Queen-to-be, the other fairies cheer. They know that it will be a long, long time before their Queen is ready to leave them, but the ways of Fairyland will be safe when that day comes.

"To think that I was named on the day the new Queen was found," cries Skysinger. "I will never forget this."

And the fairy choir, which has been huddling behind a tree trunk for the last few minutes, suddenly bursts into song:

Fairies of the earth and sky,
Dance and sing,
Flit and fly.
Follow one,
Follow all,
To this happy Blossom Ball.

Fairies of the night and day,
Twist and twirl,
Laugh and play.
Follow one,
Follow all,
To this happy Blossom Ball.

Fairies of the sea and land,
Fluttering here,
Hand in hand.
Follow one,
Follow all,
To this happy Blossom Ball.

Fairies of the stream and wood,
Greet your Queen,
Wise and good.
Follow one,
Follow all,
To this happy Blossom Ball.

Fairy first, fairy last,
Past and future
Meet at last.
Follow one,
Follow all,
To this happy Blossom Ball.

The Fruits of
the Forest

On a warm, soft, summer day, when the golden fields are splashed with poppies, and the apple-tree branches begin to bend with the weight of their shining fruits, the fairies meet to talk about the special time to come. We might call it the harvest, but to the fairies it is and always has been … the Gathering.

Summer is a slow and sleepy time in Fairyland. Little fairies wander through the flowers, learning their names and watching how the bees and butterflies busy themselves among the bright petals. Older fairies make midsummer magic, sending sunshine spells to ripen fruit on trees and in hedgerows. They love to feel the warm breezes in their hair and sit unseen among the leaves, watching the little fairies flitting happily below. As the shadows lengthen on perfect afternoons, it is impossible to imagine the dark days of winter.

But nothing stays the same
for ever, and the fairies know
that summer will slowly turn
to autumn. It is time for the fruits
of the forest to be collected, to feed the tiny
creatures of the woodlands and fields during
the long, cold days to come.

And so, one sunny day, the Gathering begins.
Fairies from far and wide come together to plan
this most important time – and to talk about the
party they will have when the hard work is
done. In a glade in the middle of a wood, where
patches of sunlight dapple the mossy floor, fairy
voices, like tiny tinkling bells, are heard.

"Fairies! Attention!" calls a silvery voice, but the chatter of dozens of little people, who are busy greeting friends and relations they have not seen since last year's Gathering, goes on.

"Fairies!" The voice becomes more steely than silvery. One or two fairies look up, but many more are much too busy to notice.

The Fairy Queen signals to a tiny boy in blue, who lifts to his lips a stripy snail's shell and makes an amazingly loud noise.

At once, all is quiet in the glade, except for the buzzing of the honey bees. They never can keep quiet, even for a minute.

"Fairy friends!" cries the Fairy Queen. "We are pleased to see so many of you here today. Later, there will be time for fun and frolics, but now, we have a huge job to do. This year, our task is bigger than ever. The gentle rains and warm sunny days have done their work. Now it is our turn. Have you chosen your teams?"

At once, there is confusion again, as fairies flit and fly here, there and everywhere. But in a moment, they are grouped in neat rows and sitting cross-legged on the ground.

"Fruits and Berries!" calls the Queen. "Are you ready?"

"We are!" calls a jolly band of fairies in costumes of purple, blue and red.

"Excellent," replies their leader. "Now, this year I want good, quick picking – and *no* squirting!" The year before, some smaller fairies discovered that if they jumped hard on blackberries and blueberries, spurts of juice would shoot out and splash their friends. It was fantastic fun – until a Feather Fairy got hit by mistake and complained to the Queen.

"Field Fairies, are you all gathered?" asks the Queen now, and a host of golden fairies flutters up. They are ready to search the fields for the ripe grains that farmers let fall.

One by one, the Queen names her forces: the copper crew who bring home nuts and seeds; the pale, floating fairies who gather thistledown and dandelion clocks; the bustling brown workers who tackle the larger items, such as chestnuts and acorns; the speedy, copper crew who catch the falling leaves that have a special magic if they never touch the ground.

When the gleaners and gatherers are ready, one last group is left. These are recorders, who scratch tiny marks on bark and stones to note the totals of this year's Gathering.

All the fairies turn their pretty faces to the Queen. There is a moment's hush and then, smiling, she claps her little hands. A cloud of fairies hovers for a second in the air – and is gone. The Gathering has begun.

Alone in the glade, the Queen is just about to sit down to plan the Gathering Party, when she hears a tiny sound. A little fairy voice can be heard nearby, muttering sadly. But surely, all the fairies have flown away?

Hidden behind the gnarled root of a tree, the Queen finds a little figure, head in hands.

"My dear," she says, "what is the matter?"

The little fairy jumps and is even more frightened when she realizes who is talking.

"Oh, Your Highness," she says, "I'm so, so sorry."

"But why, my dear?" asks the Queen. "Don't be upset."

The whole story comes tumbling out.

"I was caught in a c-cobweb," says the fairy, "and couldn't get here on time. Now I won't be able to help with the G-G-Gathering. And I'll miss the p-p-party!"

"Nonsense," says the Queen. "I was just wondering who I could find to help me organize things. The others will be tired when they have finished. You are just the fairy I need. Come on … there is lots to do."

For the next few days, while the countryside hums with the sound of fairy wings, the Queen and her little helper prepare the glade. They sew garlands of feathers and flowers to hang from the branches. They talk nicely to the fireflies and glow-worms about making chains of tiny lights among the trees. They make acorn cups and walnut-shell bowls, and scatter petals for fairies to sit on.

"Now," laughs the Queen, "we must talk to the spiders. They make lovely, lacy hammocks for tired fairies to rest in."

"Sp-sp-spiders?" asks her little helper.
"Oh, I don't know…."

"Ah, yes, the cobweb, I remember," says the Queen, "but, you know, you'll find that spiders are not so bad."

In fact, the spiders are very kind indeed. When they hear about what happened to the little fairy, they spin a beautiful lacy dress for her to wear at the party.

It is late one afternoon by the time that everything is ready.

"Phew! Now I can rest," sighs the little fairy. But the Queen smiles. "I don't think so!" she says. "Listen!"

The sound of a hundred tiny beating wings fills the air for a second, then there is laughter and singing and chattering on every side. The party has begun!

The Uninvited
Guest

Everyone agrees that this is the best Gathering ever. The little fairies are tired but happy. Grain, nuts, berries and seeds are safely tucked away in hundreds of tiny hiding places. Now it is time to celebrate that one more Gathering has been successfully completed.

As the sun sinks, the fireflies and glow-worms take up their positions to light the perfect party.

There is food and drink for everyone. Some small fairies eat so much that they have to have a nap among the rose petals. Fairy musicians, playing reed flutes, acorn drums, snail-shell horns and seed-pod shakers, soon have toes tapping and wings flapping. If you have never seen a fairy dance, you have missed a wonderful sight.

Fairies, you see, dance on the ground as lightly and delicately as thistledown, but they can dance in the air, too. Their wings shimmer behind them as they twirl.

From her throne at the base of a mighty oak tree, the Queen smiles at the pretty sight and thanks each fairy who comes to curtsey or bow before her.

The highlight of any fairy party is always the dance called the Daisy Chain.

Everyone dances it, from the tiniest little fairy to the Queen herself. Holding hands, the fairies form an enormous ring and follow each other in an intricate pattern, dancing in and out, up and down, around and around.

As the Daisy Chain becomes faster and faster, fairies laugh breathlessly, their eyes and cheeks bright with pleasure. Everything is perfect until …

Tooooo! Tooooo! Whoooo
is making this noise?

The deafening voice comes from high in the oak tree. As the fairies flutter to the ground in confusion, a huge bird glides into the glade on silent wings and settles on a low branch. His bright, round eyes shine in the darkness. It is an owl!

Now fairies are gentle people. They try to be friendly to their fellow creatures. But they are often afraid of owls. They know that they are mysterious birds, who fly at night without a single flutter to betray their presence. They know, too, that owls eat other tiny creatures. Their beaks and claws are sharp and swift. It is not surprising that fairies keep their distance.

As usual, it is the Queen who takes charge. Boldly, she marches towards the owl and speaks up in a clear, courageous voice. "We are holding our Gathering Party," she cries. "It is a tradition with us. We do not wish to disturb other creatures. Pray, whom do I have the honour of addressing?"

The owl bows his head. "I am Strix, Madam," he hoots. "I live in this great tree. Yooooou understand, the night is my own time, when I can come and goooo in peace as I please."

"I am sorry we have troubled you," says the Queen of the Fairies. "We shall be gone by dawn. In the meantime, won't you join our party?"

"Noooo," replies Strix more loudly. "That will not dooo. Look up! What do you see?"

"Why, nothing," says the Queen with a frown. "How strange. The moon has gone!"

"It is covered by a dark cloud, Madam. A huge storm is coming. You and your people could be blown away."

The fairies shiver and hug each other when they hear this news. How can they all find shelter so far from home and in the dark, too? Their fear must show on the Queen's face, as well, for the owl's fierce stare softens a little.

"My tree," he says, "is ancient indeed. It is holloooow. There is plenty of roooom for all of yooou inside." For a moment, it almost seems as if he smiles. "Nearly roooom," he hoots, "for a party!"

In no time at all, the little fairies clamber and flutter through the hole in the trunk of the old oak tree that the owl shows them. The fireflies and the glow-worms come too, filling the shelter with golden light. In this warm, safe place, the fairy musicians soon strike up a tune, and happy faces are seen once more.

Only the Queen, standing by the opening, sees the ragged

moon appear through the clouds. She watches as the branches bow before a cold, whipping wind, and sees the first heavy, drenching drops spoil the scattered petals the fairies have left behind.

The Queen smiles sadly. It is the same every year. After the warm, welcoming days of the Gathering, winter is never far behind. The raindrops are his messengers, warning that it is time for all fairies to find their way home.

"Always a little sad, is it not soooo?" whispers a voice from a branch high above.

"And happy, too," whispers the Queen in return. "The seasons only leave to come again."

"Ah, Madam," sighs the owl, "soooo true. Soooo true."

A Winter's
Journey

When the cold, dark days of winter come, there is only one thing for fairies to do. They find themselves a cosy home and stay inside until the first signs of spring send them scurrying out to be busy in the world again. It is during this cosy time that fairies tell the old stories of Fairyland and sing the enchanted songs of long ago.

Finding a safe place to spend the winter is the first thing a fairy thinks about after the fun of the Gathering in autumn. Some fairies like an abandoned bird's nest, lined with soft, warm feathers. Others prefer a hole in a tree, or the nooks and crannies under the gnarled roots of ancient trees. Wherever they choose, fairies make sure that they have friends and family with them. No fairy likes to be alone – for how are the old tales to be told without an audience?

Although fairies prefer not to go outside in the cold weather, other creatures can still be seen in the winter woodland. Bright-eyed birds, in particular, hop about the bare branches. They bring news of the outside world to the fairies and, as they are terrible gossips, soon pass on snippets of information about other fairy groups. And that is how the terrible news of the Queen's illness spread among the little folk.

The Queen herself always spends the winter in a mossy cave on a hillside. It is really just the space made where one boulder has rolled against another, but it makes a grand and comfortable home for the most important fairy of all. Here the Queen is safe and warm in the worst weather, though outside the rain and wind are wild and cold.

But a day comes when the Queen feels that the cold is no longer outside but in her own tiny body. She shivers and coughs and wraps herself in a blanket of thistledown. A heavy sadness comes over her. It is no good. By the evening, the Queen is really ill, and the fairies hovering around her can do nothing to help.

"Tell the others!" a little fairy peeps out from the cave to tell a robin perching above. "We don't know what to do, but perhaps one of the fairy folk will be able to help. Go quickly, please!"

The robin flies off, eager to take his news to all the fairies hidden in the winter world.

Now fairies are hardly ever ill. Living as they do in the open air and the sunlight, with all the good things of the earth to eat, they are usually full of laughter and liveliness. As news of the Queen's illness flies from burrow to nest, all the fairies are worried. They simply do not know what to do.

"Sunshine is what she needs," say several fairies.
"And good spring water."

69

"There'll be no sunshine this month," another fairy replies, looking up at the leaden skies. "I'd say we're expecting snow and lots of it!"

It is not until a day later that a little fairy called Merrydown hears of the Queen's sickness. "Tell me everything," she begs the bird who brings the news. "Is she pale? Does she have a fever? Is she sleepy?"

The messenger bird tells the fairy everything he knows, but there is a lot he cannot be sure about. Merrydown crawls back into the bird's nest where she is spending the winter with her friends and tells them what she has heard.

"I was thinking," she says, her eyes shining, "of the sunbeam we caught last summer."

"It would be just the thing!" cries her friend Fern. "We will be in the dark," she adds regretfully, "but the Queen should have it. Only how will we get it to her? It's too delicate for a bird with a big, clumsy beak to carry."

Merrydown is determined. "I'll take it," she says. "I know it's a long way, but I can carry it carefully and, anyway, on the way there the sunbeam itself will keep me warm."

The little fairies look up at the ceiling of the nest. Shining above them is something golden, glowing within a lantern made of closely woven cobwebs. One glorious day of sunshine, a few months before, the fairies were lucky enough to catch a sunbeam that shone through the leaves on to the woodland floor. It has kept them warm all winter, but now it is time to give it to someone who needs it more.

So it is that Merrydown sets off on the Great Journey that fairies still speak of. Fairies cannot fly in the winter, when there is no warmth to smooth their wings, so Merrydown has to walk. Even in her cloak of feathers and clutching the sunbeam, she feels the cold.

Merrydown sets out very early one morning, when the grey sky is flushed with pink and orange. She walks without stopping all morning and into the afternoon. It is hard. She has to scramble over rocks and branches without using her wings or her hands, which are carefully holding the sunbeam.

By about two o'clock, her feet are dirty and sore, and the cold is beginning to bite at her tiny toes. Merrydown does not need to think about which direction to take. All fairies can always find their Queen – it is a kind of instinct they have.

Then, just as Merrydown is thinking she must find somewhere to rest, something terrible happens. It begins to snow. Huge, soft flakes come thick and fast out of the sky. It seems darker, and Merrydown now feels the cold trickling down her neck and settling on her head and shoulders. She shivers and stumbles, and, as she does so, she drops the sunbeam!

Paralysed with horror, Merrydown watches the glow bouncing gently down the slope in front of her, leaving no impression on the light covering of snow. With a cry, the little fairy tumbles down the hill after the light, fearing at any moment to see it break on a rock and spill out into the gathering gloom.

But the light rolls on until it drops – *plop* – into a little river at the bottom of the slope. Merrydown gives a wail as she sees it bobbing away in the fast-running water.

"Jump on if you want to catch it!" hisses a voice in her ear. To the fairy's astonishment, a beautiful swan rises up out of the snow, where it has been almost hidden.

Merrydown doesn't have time to think. She jumps on to the bird's white feathers and settles down among them. The dark water rushes them along as the snow continues to fall. At last, as the day grows darker still, Merrydown realizes that the water has become calm. The river has emptied into a large lake, and the sunbeam is bobbing gently on the water only a few inches away.

"You had better stay here tonight," says the swan. "You are so light I can hardly feel you. Sleep on my back, and I will watch the light for you. In the morning, I will set you on the bank and you can go on."

The tired fairy lays down her heavy head and is soon dreaming beneath the night sky. The snow stops falling, and the merest sliver of a silvery moon rises in the sky.

The next day, Merrydown sets off on foot again. She can feel that the Queen is closer now. It has been much quicker to travel by water than by land. At last, reaching the top of a high hill, Merrydown knows that she is very close indeed. Eagerly, she runs forward – and completely loses her footing on the slippery slope. This time, the fairy holds on to the light, clutching it to her as she skids through the snow and comes to a stop ... just outside the Queen's winter cave.

Hardly daring to breathe, Merrydown creeps inside. The sunbeam lights up a sad scene. There lies the Queen, pale and still on a bed of swan's down. Around her, the fairy court looks near to tears.

Merrydown doesn't waste a moment. Quickly pulling a leaf curtain across the entrance to the cave, she gently releases the sunbeam. At once, the sunshine in all its brightness springs out into the room, lighting up every corner and bringing a golden glow to the Queen's lovely face.

At once, she opens her eyes and sits up. "Oh, I feel so much better!" she cries. "It's as if the summer has come. Thank you, my dear!" All around, fairies beam and bustle, hurrying to bring food and comforts to their welcome visitor.

It is soon decided that it is too dangerous for Merrydown to make the return journey without the sunbeam, so she stays by the Queen's side for the rest of the winter.

The Secrets of
the Snow

The snow that begins to fall when Merrydown makes her Great Journey stops only for a little while. Then it begins again and does not cease for a whole week. As far as the eye can see, the world is white. Heavy blankets of snow lie on the branches of the great trees in the wood and bow down the smaller plants. The lakes and ponds are frozen, and only a small trickle of water still flows in the icy streams and rivers. The snow dampens many sounds, so that the world seems strangely quiet and still.

For many weeks, the weather is icy cold. Although the sun shines brightly on the snow by day, there is no thaw. Very few animals venture out. There is nothing for them to eat, and they are better snugly sleeping in their holes and burrows. Only the bright-eyed birds hop around from time to time, leaving their spiky footprints in the snow.

Most fairies, cosy in their winter homes, do not dream of venturing out. A very little snow can bury a fairy, and, as you know, they cannot fly in the wintertime. But one little band of friends is excited by the winter wonderland and wants to feel what it is like in a frosty world.

"As light as they are, fairies can sink into soft snow," warns a Flower Fairy. "You must never go out when the weather is like this. It is far too dangerous."

But to the little fairies, who have not yet been given the tasks they will perform in the outside world, the spring and summer seem a long way away. They want to discover the secrets of nature now. They long to explore the fascinating world outside the old tree trunk in which they live.

One day, the smallest little fairy of all has an idea.

"It wouldn't be going outside exactly," he says. "It would be kind of being inside outside."

"What are you talking about?" the other fairies laugh. "You're not making any sense at all, Shimmer."

But Shimmer knows what he means and he starts to explain. "Where there's a hole, just at the bottom of the trunk," he says, "the snow is pushed right up against the tree. This morning, I touched it and, you know, it's really soft."

"We know *that*," sigh the other little fairies. "So what?"

"You can easily dig it with your hands," replies Shimmer.

Now he has their attention. They look at him with bright little eyes and start to have Big Ideas.

"So you mean we could dig some away …" says Shine.

"And make a sort of tunnel …" says Glitter.

"And go adventuring *inside* the snow!" finishes Sparkle. "Let's do it!"

The little fairies have half an idea that bigger fairies might try to stop them if they know, so they keep quiet about their plan and scuttle down to the roots of the tree where the hole is. Shimmer is quite right. The snow is very easy to dig with their hands, if a little cold. Then Shine makes another discovery.

"You don't really have to dig," she says. "Look, you can sort of push the snow together, so it gets harder. That way, there's no dug-out snow to get rid of."

The others find that she is right, and before the morning is over, they have made quite a long tunnel away from the tree trunk and across the clearing. It isn't very big – just wide enough for a fairy to tiptoe along. And it isn't dark, either, because somehow light from above seems to glow through the snow.

The little fairies just love their new playground. Over the next few days they hollow out more tiny tunnels and even little rooms under the surface of the snow.

Then, one morning, Glitter suddenly falls through a hole into another tunnel! She realizes that she has come round in a circle and found the first tunnel. Now the little fairies can enjoy games of chase all day long.

It is Sparkle who makes the next big discovery. Her tiny hands suddenly touch something rough and warmer than the snow. When she clears more of the white, powdery stuff away, she finds that she has come to another tree trunk. And inside, there is another group of little fairies, who are very surprised indeed to have visitors in the middle of a snowy, blowy winter!

It isn't long before all the fairies in both tree trunks know about what the little fairies have been doing, but they cannot be angry. It is so nice to be able to go visiting through the snow!

Soon there are dozens of tunnels criss-crossing the clearing and travelling further afield, too. The fairies have never had such a festive time, visiting their neighbours, finding treasures in the snow tunnels, and enjoying a whole new wintertime adventure.

"We shall call you the Frost Fairies," the grown-ups tell the little fairies who started it all.

Then, one fine morning, a fairy is walking along the tunnel to visit her friend on the other side of the clearing when something very worrying happens. *Plop!* A big drop of water lands right on her head!

At first, the fairy cannot believe what has happened, but when she touches her hair and looks at her dripping dress, she cannot be in doubt. She runs quickly back to her own tree and calls, "It's raining in the tunnel! What shall we do?"

"Wait a minute," replies an older, wiser fairy. "It can't be raining in the tunnel. It must be something else." And, as they sit thinking, all of them at once suddenly realize what is happening. It's the thaw! The snow is melting!

"Our little ones are in danger!" cries the first fairy. "We must make sure that no one is in the tunnels. They could drown in the drips! There could be puddles! What if the roof of a tunnel collapses while our babies are underneath? Oh, what can we do?"

"We need to sound a fairy warning," says the older, wiser fairy, whose name is Berry. "Where is the snail's shell? Now, find me some big, shiny leaves. Holly would be fine."

Later that afternoon, Berry sets off along the tunnels, wearing on his head an extraordinary hat made of holly leaves. It is a clever idea. If icy water drips on to his head, it slides off the shiny leaves and falls to the floor on either side. And all the time he walks along, Berry blows the snail's-shell bugle. Fairies hurry from the tunnels, knowing that something is wrong.

Soon, everyone is safely at home, and the danger is past.

"We must be careful next year," says Shimmer, "and work out a way to warn other fairies when the tunnels are no longer safe. How sad it is that we won't be able to play in them any more this year."

Berry grins. "Don't be silly," he says. "Don't you realize what this means? The snow is melting! We will be able to go outside again. The world is waking up. It will soon be spring!"

For days, the fairies wait, listening to the *drip! drop!* of snow melting on the branches and the big *schloop!* when a whole branchful of snow slides to the ground. It begins to feel warmer, and one day the snow melts enough for a little weak sunlight to filter through a crack in the trunk and light up the inside.

"Do you think …?" asks Shine.

"Not quite yet," says Berry, but he is smiling.

Then, one morning, the little fairies wake early. At first, they cannot understand why. Then they know. All around them, out in the wide world, birds are singing. From every branch, there comes a busy, twittering, tweeting, joyful sound.

One by one, the fairies creep outside. It is cool still, but the sun is shining, and the birds are fluttering and flirting in the branches.

"Oh, but look," says Glitter. "There is still some snow over there."

"Not snow," smiles Berry. "Snowdrops! The first flowers of spring. Another beautiful year has begun."

The Dreamland Fairies

A Dream for Everyone

Imagine a place that is very, very far away – and very, very near at the same time. Imagine a place that is always busy, and always peaceful. Imagine a place that is everywhere, and nowhere. It's difficult, isn't it? And yet, you have been there yourself. It is called Dreamland.

It is easy to visit Dreamland. You won't need a car or a bus or a plane. But you mustn't try too hard to get there, or it will suddenly, silently disappear!

The Dreamland fairies live there all the time, of course. They work hard to bring you the dreams you want and the dreams you need. And to do their work well, they have to be really, really good at

dreaming!

Dreams are very special. They can take you anywhere you like and bring you safely home again in time for a brand new day. So how do the Dreamland fairies do their important work? Let me explain ...

The best way to show you how dreams are made, is to find someone who needs a dream right now. Let's see. Far away from Dreamland, but very near at the same time, the sun is just setting behind a hill, and the sky is turning from orange, to pink, to purple.

On the edge of a nearby wood, someone needs a dream. In fact, lots of someones need dreams tonight.

Under the roots of an old hawthorn tree, Mrs Matilda Rabbit is putting her little ones to bed. There are five of them!

Up in the branches above, Mr Benjamin Bird is settling his three chicks down for the night.

By a little stream, running close by, Great Aunt Phoebe Frog is trying to persuade her lively great-nephew to snuggle down in his bed of weeds and cool, comfy mud.

"Sweet dreams, Chick One, Chick Two, and Chick Three!" coos Mr Bird, as he pulls a piece of moss around his little ones. (Mr Bird is still thinking about names for his nestlings.)

"Sweet dreams, Rodney, Rosie, Rickie, Radish, and Snoople!" calls Mrs Rabbit, as she closes the bedroom door.

"Sweet Dreams, Glurgle!" croaks Great Aunt Phoebe, and pushes him firmly into the squelchy mud.

And from the bedroom, and the nest, and the muddy, froggy bed, little dream-wishes rise up into the air. You can hardly see them but, like tiny bubbles, they drift up, up, up ... and pop with a *ping!* in Dreamland.

Ping! A little fairy wakes, knowing at once that a very wet and weedy dream is needed for a sleepy froglet.

Ping! An older fairy understands that three little chicks want to share a dream tonight.

Ping! Ping! Ping! Ping! Ping! A group of fairy friends has a lot to do! Those wriggling rabbits have all got very different ideas about the dreams they need.

The dream for a froglet is not hard for even a small fairy to organize. Fairy Rose flies off into Dreamland at once. She soon comes to a big, beautiful lake, where dragonflies hover above deep, cool water, and water lilies bloom like stars across the shining surface.

Fairy Rose does not like swimming. She stands at the edge of the lake and calls out in her silvery voice. "Samuel! Are you there?"

Almost at once, a little golden fish pops up his head. "How can I help?" he asks cheerfully. "It's a dream for a young frog, Sammy," Fairy Rose explains.

"You don't have to explain," groans the fish. "All frogs want to dream about is chasing fish like me. I've done this a dozen times. Just leave it to me. What's the name of the young fellow?"

Fairy Rose tells him and flies off with a wave and a happy smile. That was an easy job. She knows that Samuel will swim through Glurgle's dreams until morning, making the froglet happy and giving Great Aunt Phoebe the peaceful night she deserves.

Finding a dream for little birds to share is trickier, but Fairy Fern knows that those little birds are nearly ready to fly. An exciting flying dream is just what they need.

Fairy Fern goes to see a butterfly friend. "I need a dream for three birds to share," she explains. "I'd like some gentle flying to put them in the mood for their father's lessons tomorrow. I know he is worried."

"Then perhaps you should be finding a dream for him!" the butterfly laughs. "I'm sorry, I can't help you tonight. I have already agreed to appear in a bunny's dream."

A dragonfly sighs sadly. "No, I'm resting my wings tonight, I'm afraid." Several little birds are also already busy. "You could ask the hawk," they chirp.

Fairy Fern is afraid the hawk will frighten Mr Bird's little ones. She is upset that she can't find a flying friend to help. Then one of the little birds she has asked flies after her. "Why don't you do it yourself, Fairy Fern? You can fly!"

The little fairy laughs, and all night long, in the little birds' dreams, she flutters and flaps, whizzes and zooms, so that they just can't wait to fly themselves.

Now for those sleeping bunnies. They are all such different little bunnies that they all want different kinds of dreams. And bunnies are impatient. That's why they bounce around so much. It's no good waiting until the sun is slipping up into the sky again before they each have a good dream. Three fairy friends have some quick thinking to do.

Fairy Bluebell closes her eyes to concentrate on the dream wishes floating up towards her. "Rodney Rabbit wants to dream about pirates," she says, "and Rosie Rabbit would love to be a ballerina. Rickie and Radish are very keen on jumping. They want to be winners in the Rabbit Olympics. As for Snoople, I don't understand what he wants to dream about at all!"

Fairy Mallow closes her eyes, too. "You're right," she says. "I don't understand a thing that is going on in that young bunny's head. He can't really be wanting to dream about dust, can he?"

"Nobody wants to dream about dust," giggles Fairy Lime. "Let me try." She closes her eyes and laughs. "He doesn't want to dream about dust," she says. "He has tumbled out of bed and crawled underneath it. The dust under the bed is tickling his nose and ... oh, dear ... he has sneezed and woken up all his brothers and sisters. Poor Mrs Rabbit is settling them down again."

While a frazzled rabbit mother persuades her babies to go back to sleep, the fairies set to work. Fairy Bluebell doesn't much like flying over the Dreamland sea in search of pirates, but she is lucky to find Captain Thunder-thump, the most famous pirate of them all, on dry land. He is dealing with the woodworm in his leg.

"Captain, would you have time for a quick bit of swash-buckling this evening?" she asks. "I know a young rabbit who would love to meet you."

The pirate shakes his fist as the last woodworm crawls away and nods his head. "I haven't anything better to do tonight," he says. "Do you mind if I bring my friend Blood-thirsty Battling Bertha?"

"Not at all," agrees Fairy Bluebell. "I don't suppose she does ballet dancing, does she?"

Bloodthirsty Battling Bertha strides into the room at just that moment. It doesn't look as if she owns a tutu. Fairy Bluebell hopes her friends are having better luck.

Meanwhile, Fairy Mallow has tried to persuade several kangaroos, a couple of grasshoppers and whole families of frogs to help with a dream for Rickie and Radish. All are already busy. With the Rabbit Olympics so soon, Rickie and his brother are not the only two rabbits keen on jumping.

"There's only one answer," sighs Mallow, "but Mrs Rabbit isn't going to like it."

Fairy Lime finds not one bunny ballerina but a whole company looking for an audience. And since Snoople now seems to want a very noisy dream, she brings along the whole orchestra, too.

Five little bunnies spend a very happy night, but Fairy Mallow is right about Mrs Rabbit. When she hears that Rickie and Radish have spent several hours dreaming about athletic fleas, she is very cross. "I shall write a letter to the Dreamland Council," she says. "What kind of a dream is that to give young, impressionable rabbits?"

As for the Dreamland fairies, their work is far from done. For them, as dreamers in one part of the world are waking up, sleepy little ones across the ocean are settling down to sleep … and dream, of course.

A Dream
for
Dragons

On a perfect pink cloud in Dreamland, Fairy Snowflake is dreaming of frosty forests and sparkling streams, when she is suddenly woken by a dream wish that pops near her ear with a little puff of smoke!

"Oh," cries Snowflake, "this dream wish feels hot! I don't like it at all!"

She closes her eyes to concentrate on what the dreamer needs, then quickly opens them again in surprise. The sleepy wish is from a dragon!

"I can't find a dream for a dragon!" cries the fairy. "I don't know where to start!" She even tries (and Dreamland fairies really are not supposed to do this) to pretend she hasn't received the wish. But a dragon's wishes are very fierce. More and more dream wishes float up towards her, each hotter and more urgent than the one before.

"Help! I need the Dreamland Council!" cries the fairy. And she flies off at once to find the cloud where the council meets.

Fairy Snowflake is so nervous, standing before the wise fairies and elves of the Dreamland Council that her words come out in little scattered flurries, like snow.

"Slowly, slowly, my dear," says a kind old wizard. "You will need to tell us all about the dreamer before we can help you to find a dream."

The Snowflake Fairy closes her eyes and concentrates. "Oh, I don't like it!" she cries. "There are three dragons. They live in … in a cave under a volcano. Oh!"

"What is it?" asks the wizard. "Don't be afraid. Dream wishes cannot hurt you. Just tell us clearly."

Fairy Snowflake is not happy. "They want horrible dreams!" she says. "I can't do this! Oh, help me!"

The kindly wizard smiles. "I can feel these dream wishes, too," he says. "You know, these are just the kinds of dreams that dragons like to have. You love to dream of cool, white snow and frosty air. Dragons love treasure and adventure and fire! There is nothing for you to fear. I have an idea. Come with me."

"My name is Longbeard," the wizard explains. "I am going to take you to see a friend of mine. I'm afraid I can't fly like you, so we'll have to travel by magic carpet. I hope you don't mind. It's old-fashioned, I know, but sometimes the old ways are the best."

Snowflake nods vaguely. She has no idea what a magic carpet is. The next instant, she finds herself sitting on a rug that is hovering in space. It looks very old. Snowflake is pretty sure she sees a moth fluttering out of it. She also thinks it is a little bit, well, *smelly*.

Wizard Longbeard settles down happily beside her. "This is the only way to travel!" he cries. "Now I need to concentrate for a moment." He shuts his eyes and starts to mumble. Snowflake wonders if he has fallen asleep. Suddenly, the rug gives a terrifying lurch and shoots off

Suddenly, the rug gives a terrifying lurch and shoots off at incredible speed through Dreamland. Snowflake screams. "I'm going to fall! Help!"

"It only feels like that," cries Wizard Longbeard. "The carpet would never let you fall off. Smile, my dear. You'll soon start to enjoy the ride."

But before Snowflake has a chance to enjoy anything, the rug screeches to a stop as suddenly as it started. It is hovering outside the window of a large, dilapidated and rather blackened castle. The owner is at home!

Well, several unfortunate things happen all at once. Snowflake screams at the sight of the dragon. The dragon rears back in shock and hits his head on the edge of the window. In pain, he lets out a bellow of his own, and with it comes a fierce rush of flames. Wizard Longbeard yells, "Help! My carpet is on fire!" and quickly says a spell for rain.

It feels as if someone very large has thrown a bucket of water from a high window. Snowflake and the wizard land on the ground ... soaked!

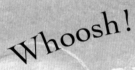

Whoosh!

"I could blow on you gently to dry you out," says a voice from above. "No!" cry two voices. For the first time, Fairy Snowflake and Wizard Longbeard are thinking the same thing.

The dragon appears in a nearby doorway. "I won't even breathe, I promise!" he says, and he looks so sorry that even Snowflake smiles. "I'm afraid we haven't made a very good start," says the dragon. "My name is Ashe. How can I help you?"

"Well, we came because my friend here is frightened of dragons," says the wizard. "This was perhaps not my best ever idea!" Suddenly, with a spluttering and snorting, he begins to laugh. It isn't long before Snowflake and Ashe are laughing, too. And it just shows what a very nice dragon he is that not even a whiff of steam comes from his mouth and nose.

Together, Fairy Snowflake and Wizard Longbeard
explain about the dragon dream.

"Well, of course, I know exactly what they want to
dream about," says Ashe. "Treasure and adventure and
frightening a few knights and their pages. Would you
like me to sort this out for you?"

"Would you?" gasps Snowflake.

"Could you?" asks Longbeard. "No real fighting, mind,
and no one must get hurt. I know what you dragons
are like when you start dreaming."

"I promise," says Ashe in a little voice, looking like a naughty puppy. "Well, I must make a start."

Extraordinarily gracefully, he rises into the air. "We must set off for home," says Longbeard, then looks doubtfully at the singed carpet.

"I could give you a lift!" calls the dragon.

So that is how a snowflake fairy has two exciting flights in one night, without flapping her own wings at all. And three dragons under a volcano have the best dreams of their lives without hurting anyone.

A Dream
for
Mermaids

Deep beneath the sea
is a wonderful world
where bright little fishes
swish and swirl, seaweed
sways with the tide, and
mermaids comb their hair
in the blue waters.

It is a dreamy world, so
perhaps you think that the
kinds of dreams we have are not
needed. That's not true. Even
octopuses dream, and mermaids are
the greatest dreamers of all, as this
story shows.

One sleepy afternoon, a water fairy is resting on a raincloud when a dream bubble pops near her ear and out jumps a little fish! Water fairies do not have wings, but they can dive through the air and sea like birds. The water fairy picks up the fish and dives gracefully into the water far below.

With a smile, the water fairy lets the little fish swim off through the clear, blue water. "Now," she wonders, "where is the mermaid who sent that dream wish?"

The water fairy, whose name is Marina, swims gently through the water, enjoying the beautiful scene. Then, behind a rock, she sees a stream of yellow hair rippling in the current. A mermaid is sitting there.

Now dream fairies do not usually make themselves known to the people and animals whose dreams they are helping to create. You haven't ever met *your* dream fairy, have you? But Marina is looking worried. She can tell, even without seeing her face, that the mermaid behind the rock is crying.

Dream fairies are very good at sensing another person's feelings – that's why they are so good at finding just the right dream. It wouldn't be easy for you or me to tell if a mermaid is crying. You can't see tears underwater. But Marina knows, and she hates to see such unhappiness.

Marina can't help herself. She swims over to the mermaid and asks, "My dear, are you all right?"

The mermaid looks up with a face that would melt the heart of a hungry shark. "I miss them so," she sobs. "I miss my family." And she is so upset that her tears fall as pearls onto the sandy seabed.

"Where is your family?" asks Marina gently, trying not to let the mermaid see her too clearly.

The mermaid sighs. "They are on the other side of the southern ocean," she says. "I agreed to come here to serve the mer-queen, and my parents and sisters were so proud that I was chosen, but I miss them terribly. I cannot let them know, though. They would be so disappointed in me."

"Certainly, they would be sorry to know that you were unhappy," Marina agrees. "You send them messages, I suppose?"

"Oh yes," says the mermaid. "I send messages by all the little fish who pass, but I try to sound happy, and it is not the same as seeing their lovely faces again."

"Of course not!" Marina is already beginning to have an idea, but she needs to consult the Dream Council before she can go ahead with her plan. She gently says goodbye to the mermaid and swims up towards the surface.

It is only when she has disappeared from view that the mermaid suddenly realizes that the kind stranger did not have a tail!

Out in the open air again, Marina soars upward to the clouds where the Dream Council meets.

A fairy greets her as she arrives. "How can we help you, water fairy?"

"I wish," says Marina slowly, "at least, I should like, well…" The fairy urges her on with a smile. "I want," Marina says in a rush, "to do something that is not allowed!"

"You had better come and tell us all about it," says the fairy gravely. Marina fears that she looks a little shocked.

A few minutes later, having heard Marina's story, the wise fairies and wizards of the Dream Council are looking calmly at her.

"You know," says one, "that we have our rules for a reason. You cannot send a dream to someone unless they have asked for it. Human beings often do not know themselves well enough to realize that they have asked for a dream, so their dreams are often surprises for them, but it is different with mermaids. Only the mermaid you met has asked for a dream. You cannot send dreams to her family as well."

Marina hangs her head. "But it would make them all so happy," she says. "If they cannot be together in their daily lives, surely they can be together in their dreams."

The members of the Dream Council look at each other. "We need some time to discuss this," they say. "Could you wait on that cloud over there?"

Marina feels a little spark of hope warming her. She had expected the Council simply to say no. It is agony waiting on the cloud, so she tries to pass the time by counting the dream bubbles that float up beside her.

At last, the friendly fairy Marina met when she arrived flutters over. "The Council is ready to talk to you now," she says.

An old wizard speaks for everyone else. "Well, you have given us an interesting problem," he says. "Dreams are very special things. We still do not think that you can send a dream to someone who has not asked for it. Still, we like your idea, so there is only one answer. You will have to make sure the other mermaids far across the sea *do* ask to dream about the mer-queen's maid."

"However am I going to do that?" asks Marina, but the wizard smiles. "Ah, that is your problem, not ours, my dear. Good luck!"

Marina swoops back to the ocean. She has no idea what to do next, but she knows that talking to her friends is often helpful when she cannot think what to do. She finds them playing with a dolphin near a small island. They listen carefully to what she has to say.

"The mermaid's family must have dreams, too," says Pearl, another water fairy. "But there is only one way you can find out. You will have to travel to the other side of the southern ocean to find out what kind of dreams they like."

"But it is far! Very, very far!" cries Marina. "I don't think that I can go so far."

Suddenly there is a *whoosh* of water, as the friendly dolphin jumps and spins beside her. "I will take you," he says. "Just climb on!"

So that is just what Marina does. "What an adventure!" she calls to the dolphin, but the sea is rushing by so quickly that he cannot hear her.

A long time later – but not as long as Marina imagined – the fairy and her friend arrive at a beautiful coral reef. Sitting on rocks, combing their hair and talking quietly together, are several mer-people.

They are so deep in conversation that they do not see Marina arrive. She cannot help overhearing them.

"It was right that she should go to the mer-queen," says one. "We could not hold her back. But I miss her so much I hardly know what to do."

"I know," says another. "Her messages sound so happy. I don't like to tell her we wish she was back here with us."

Marina can hardly believe her ears. All the time the little mermaid has been missing her family, her family has been missing *her*!

The water fairy glides into view and hovers in front of the mer-people. "Forgive me for interrupting you," she says, "but I heard what you said – couldn't you visit your relative?"

"Oh, it is too far," sighs a mermaid. "We have work to do here."

"I didn't mean swimming there," Marina explains. "You could visit her in your dreams." Then she swims quickly away, fearing that she has said too much.

That night, as stars twinkle over the glittering ocean, Marina sits on a cloud near the moon and waits. Suddenly, lots of little dream bubbles swirl around her as if they are dancing. They are from mer-people, wanting to dream about other mer-people, and Marina is pretty sure she knows exactly where they have come from. With a smile and a sigh of happiness, she gets to work. It is going to be a very busy night!

A Dream
for
Unicorns

Fairies live for a very, very long time. Fairy Serena is not an old fairy by any means, but she has lived for hundreds of years and helped with many, many dreams.

Nothing much surprises her these days – not rabbits asking for dreams about tap-dancing foxes, not butterflies asking for dreams about giants, not even giants asking for dreams about butterflies! But one moonlit night, as she rests comfortably on a cloud in Dreamland, Serena is very surprised indeed.

As a silvery dream bubble pops beside her, Serena sits up and says "Oh!" And then she wonders if she herself is dreaming, because the dream request that has just popped into her head is so very strange.

Serena flies around her cloud, feeling the breeze on her face and the warmth of the sun on her wings. No, she is not dreaming. She really has been asked for a dream by a unicorn!

Now you may wonder why this is odd. If rabbits can have dreams, and dragons can have dreams, and every creature that ever appeared in a storybook can have dreams, why can't a unicorn?

Well, what you may not know, but fairies know very well, is that unicorns never ever sleep. They are the most magical creatures of all, more magical even than fairies. Their magic is so powerful that they cannot sleep even if they try. Imagine a fizzy drink, full of bubbles. Those bubbles are like a unicorn's magic. They are always moving, popping, fizzing and if they ever stop – well, then it isn't a fizzy drink any more.

It's the same with unicorns. A unicorn without magic simply cannot exist.

So how can a unicorn possibly need a dream?

Fairy Serena flies thoughtfully off to find her friend Starlight. The night-time fairy is not resting or dreaming. She is sitting bolt upright on her cloud with a look of great surprise on her face.

"You'll never guess what has just happened!" she tells Serena in amazement.

But Serena has guessed already. Have you? "You've just had a dream request from a unicorn," she says. "Am I right?"

Serena and Starlight talk over what has happened.

"It's impossible," says Starlight. "Unicorns never sleep. I know that some creatures have daydreams, but those are not the same as the dreams that Dreamland fairies arrange. What can it mean?"

"If only we could ask them!" says Serena. "But we are not allowed to talk directly to dreamers. We will simply have to go down to the Forest of Enchantment and see if we can find out. It will be difficult though. Unicorns know when any other magical creature is near."

That gives Starlight an idea. "Come with me!" she cries, swooping away across the sky. "I know someone who can help us!"

Before long, the two fairies are flying through a very different sky, where dark purple clouds are gathered, and only a few fairies can be seen peeping from the shadows.

"But this is the place where bad dreams come!" cries Serena. She feels a little frightened, although she knows there is no need.

Please do not think that bad dreams and nightmares ever come from Dreamland. They do not. But Dreamland fairies can sometimes help to put right a dream that has become frightening or sad. They work hard to make sure that all dreams have happy endings. It is hard work, and Serena admires the fairies who do this. But why has her friend brought her here?

Starlight flies straight up to a beautiful fairy dressed in purple and silver.

"Starlight! How lovely to see you!" cries the fairy. "But why are you here?"

Starlight turns to Serena. "This is my friend Twilight," she explains. "She can help us to visit the unicorns without being seen."

"Ah," Twilight smiles. "You want to borrow a Cloud of Darkness."

Serena has no idea what this means, but she soon finds out. Clouds of Darkness are not really clouds at all. In fact, sometimes you can't even see them. But they hide things really well. They are like a kind of invisible mist. Have you ever not been able to find something that was right under your nose? Maybe a little Cloud of Darkness was hovering nearby for a moment!

A few minutes later, Serena and Starlight float off on their special cloud towards the Forest of Enchantment.

The forest is a truly wonderful place. Parts of it are shadowy and secret, with magical stars glittering among the trees.

Other parts seem to be lit by sunlight all the time, as if the trees themselves are glowing. Everywhere there are bright little flowers and butterflies.

The trees are magical, too. Some of them grow jewels, glinting and sparkling. Others sing as you pass by. Some bend down and stroke you gently with their branches. Many whisper your name when you are near.

Serena and Starlight hover through the forest on their cloud. It is like a magic carpet in a way. The fairies can see each other, and all the birds and animals above can see them clearly, but from underneath the cloud makes them invisible.

"There are some unicorns! Look!" whispers Serena.

Sure enough a little group of magical horses are standing in a clearing.

The fairies close their eyes so that they can hear what they are "saying". Unicorns do not actually speak, they listen to each other's thoughts. As fairies are magical, too, they can hear these thoughts if they concentrate really hard. That is why closing their eyes helps.

In a very short time, Serena and Starlight know exactly why the unicorns are asking for dreams. They fly quickly away to talk about what to do next.

"This is terrible," says Serena. "I had no idea."

You see, the unicorns need dreams because they are beginning to sleep. And they are beginning to sleep because their magical powers are fading away. Why is this happening? It is happening because children, who are almost as magical as fairies, have stopped believing in unicorns.

"There must be something we can do," gasps Serena. "This can't go on. If unicorns lose all their magic, they simply disappear. Soon there will be no unicorns at all."

Starlight nods. "This is happening because unicorns are such clever, secretive creatures," she says. "They are very good at remaining hidden. Children sometimes catch just the tiniest glimpse of a fairy, so they still believe in us, but they hardly ever see even the smallest part of a unicorn."

"Perhaps we can change that," says Serena slowly. "Are you thinking what I'm thinking?"

"You mean we could give children dreams about unicorns?" whispers Starlight. "That's an excellent idea. But, you know, we can only give dreams that are asked for. Children almost never ask for dreams about unicorns."

"That's true," Serena agrees, "but there are lots of children who wish for a dream but are not sure what they want to dream about. We could send all of them unicorn dreams."

"It is too much work for the two of us …," Starlight begins.

"Of course! We need all our friends to help!" cries Serena. "Hurry! There's no time to lose!"

So that night, fairies all over Dreamland send unicorn dreams to children everywhere. Perhaps you have had one yourself!

Meanwhile, Serena and Starlight remember the dream requests. To the unicorns they send dreams of magical hope and happiness, to help them until their own magic returns.

It is not long before children all over the world are talking about unicorns.

Some of them do not remember their dreams and wonder why unicorns have popped into their heads. All of them agree that unicorns are the most wonderful magical creatures of all. And you will be pleased to know that from that night to this, not a single Dreamland fairy has received a dream request from a unicorn.

"I love to be asked for dreams," Serena tells her friend Starlight, "but this is one time when I'm very, very glad to have no requests at all – well only from lots of children wanting dreams about unicorns, anyway!"

A Dream
for a
Wizard

One quiet evening, the Dreamland fairies are sitting
on their clouds, watching the sky turn pink and
gold and purple as the day comes to an end. Soon, they
know, pretty dream bubbles will start to rise as sleepy
little ones everywhere begin to close their eyes.

"I love this time of day," says Fairy Marigold. "It's exciting, not knowing what kind of dream requests are going to come. We never know what will happen next. That's what I love about Dreamland."

A second later, Marigold's words come true – but not in the way she meant! There is a puff of purple smoke and a silvery ringing sound. The fairies look around in surprise. Only an older fairy, Emmelina, begins to smile. "Little ones," she says, "I think we are about to have a visitor."

There is another puff of smoke. The silvery ringing becomes louder and begins to sound slightly out of tune. One or two of the fairies' clouds begin to shake and bob about in the sky.

"Whatever is happening?" cries Marigold.

"No need to worry!" replies a deep, quavery voice. "It's only me!" And all at once a strange-looking fellow in a tall hat and a cloak lands with a bump on Marigold's cloud! His long stockinged legs wave in the air as he tries to regain his balance. "I'm so sorry," he says. "My landings are getting worse and worse. Perhaps I need to retake my flying test."

Marigold hardly knows what to say, she is so surprised. But Emmelina flies over and helps the old man to sit up and straighten his hat and cloak.

"I believe I have the pleasure of greeting Wizard Moonbeam," she smiles. "You visited once when I was a very young fairy, sir, and I have always remembered you."

"Well, that is very kind of you. Very kind indeed," says the wizard. "Yes, it is some while since I was here. I felt it was time for me to visit again. I am sure that everything is in order."

Seeing the confused looks on some fairy faces, Emmelina explains. "Wizard Moonbeam comes to Dreamland every so often as an inspector," she says. "He makes sure that we are making happy dreams and that all our dreamers are pleased with them. I hope you have had no complaints, sir, since you were here last?"

"Well, not really," says the wizard. "Those pixies who live in the Higgledy Hills are always muttering and moaning, you know. It's not your fault, my dears. They are simply too silly most of the time to ask for the dreams they really want. If they will fall asleep thinking about apple pies and red nightcaps, then that is what they will dream about."

"Last week one of them wanted to dream about a pair of slippers," laughs a little fairy.

"I know," smiles the wizard. "Someone should teach those pixies how to ask for dreams properly. I suppose I will have to go over there myself one day. Now, I must get back to business."

"What would you like to see while you are here?" Emmelina asks the visitor. "Dream wishes will begin to arrive at any moment, so we shall soon be busy."

"Of course, of course," says the wizard, "and that is just as it should be. With your permission I will simply sit here and observe." Seeing the confused looks of some of the smallest fairies, he explains, "That just means that I will watch what you do and give advice if I think you need it."

No sooner has the wizard finished speaking than two or three dream bubbles float up beside the fairies.

Wizard Moonbeam watches as each dream bubble bursts
with a *ping!* beside a little fairy. "I never know," he says
with a smile, "if the bubble somehow chooses a fairy or if
it is just chance who is nearby when it bursts."

One little fairy laughs excitedly. "A little elf wants a
dream about a princess," she says. "I'm off to see Princess
Corona. She is always *so* kind. And her palace is lovely!"

"Quite right, my dear," says Wizard Moonbeam.
"A very good choice."

Another little fairy looks
puzzled. "A seagull wants a
dream about fish," she says. "I
don't really know what to do."

"Yes, you do," says Emmelina
kindly. "Where do fish live?
In the sea! And who can help
you there?"

"Oh, a water fairy!" cries the
little one. "Of course! That's
easy!" And she flies off
towards the ocean.

"Well, everything seems to be going very well here," says the
wizard. "I think you hardly need to be inspected. But, oh
dear me, whatever is the matter over there?"

On a large cloud nearby,
a little fairy dressed in
golden yellow is
sobbing as if her heart
will break.

Emmelina hurries over to help her, but the little fairy just cries harder when she sees her.

"I'm so sorry," she sobs. "I know I shouldn't have done it!"

Emmelina glances at Wizard Moonbeam. "Done what?" she asks in the gentlest voice you can imagine.

"I … I … I refused a dream request!" says the fairy. "It all happened so quickly. I didn't really mean to. It was just so silly, that's all. And I wanted to arrange a beautiful dream, so that you would be proud of me!"

Now it is an important rule in Dreamland that no dream request, no matter what it is, can be ignored. Sometimes dreams need to be changed a little bit to make them just right, but it is not the fairies' job to say whether a dream can be delivered or not. If there is any question, the Dreamland Council must be consulted.

Wizard Moonbeam cannot help looking shocked, but his voice is not unkind when he speaks. "What exactly was the dream request?" he asks.

"It was from a pixie," sobs the little fairy. Emmelina and the wizard exchange a look of understanding. "He wanted a dream about Toffo-licious-munchy-crunchies."

"About *what*?" exclaims the wizard.

"Toffo-licious-munchy-crunchies," says Emmelina. "They are a new pixie breakfast cereal. Everyone, at least everyone who's a pixie, is talking about them."

"It certainly is a very silly thing to want to dream about," says the wizard, "but as you know, my dear, that is not for us to decide. Now, I think we are going to have to go to the Higgledy Hills to sort this matter out. And I can have

a few words with those tricky pixies while we are there.
You had better come too, little one. What is your name?"

"B-Buttercup," stammers the poor fairy. "I'll never do
anything like this again. I promise!"

"I hope not," says the wizard, but his eyes are twinkling.
"Now, can we fly to the Higgledy Hills on a cloud?
My flying isn't always very reliable these days."

Emmelina soon summons up a suitable cloud, and the
three set out. The Higgledy Hills, like so many things in
Dreamland, are a long way away in the daytime but very
close by when your eyes are shut. Only a minute or two
later, the cloud hovers among the hills.

It is daytime in the Higgledy Hills, not bedtime as the fairies have imagined. Buttercup is able to lead the others to a little red doorway in a hillside. "He lives in here," she whispers.

Wizard Moonbeam knocks loudly on the door. Almost at once, it creaks open. A pixie mother is standing there, looking upset and worried.

"Excuse me, madam," says the wizard. "My name is Moonbeam. I believe your son may be having trouble sleeping."

The pixie looks surprised. "I wish he was," she says. "He sleeps all the time! Are you some kind of doctor? You'd better come in."

Inside, the little house is tidy and snug, like most pixie homes. The fairies, who think of pixies as naughty, difficult creatures, begin to feel that they may have been mistaken, especially when the pixie mother shows them to comfortable chairs and brings them nettle tea and cakes.

"I've been worried about young Ruffles for some time," she confesses, when she sits down herself. "He does nothing but sleep all day and all night. I have to wake him for mealtimes. Mind you, he seems perfectly happy and well when he is awake.

Just at that moment, a small pixie appears in the doorway. "I'm feeling a bit hungry," he says, yawning.

"Ruffles!" cries his mother. "You're awake! That's amazing!" She turns to the wizard. "Thank you, sir. And you didn't even have to see him! You must be a very clever doctor indeed."

"My dear woman, I haven't done anything," says the wizard. "I believe that my young assistant Buttercup here has done the trick. How are you feeling, young fellow?"

Ruffles scratches his nose and shrugs. "I'm fine," he says. "I don't feel like sleeping any more, that's all. In fact, I'd rather go out to play."

His mother is beaming. "That's wonderful!" she cries. "Play as long as you like, sweetheart. I'm sure your friends are down by the stream with their leaf-boats."

Ruffles hurries off at once, grabbing a cake as he goes. His mother is almost in tears. "I'm just so grateful," she says. "I've been so worried, but I didn't know what to do."

"There is nothing to worry about at all," the wizard reassures her, "but I will be giving a course of lectures in the next few weeks on the subject of sleeping and dreams. Perhaps you will bring your son along. I think that many pixies could learn something useful. But for now, we must be going."

Wizard Moonbeam and the fairies fly home on their cloud. The wizard smiles kindly at Buttercup. "I shall be giving a few lectures in Dreamland, as well," he says. "It's not that you are doing a bad job, my dears. You are doing too good a job! That young pixie had such wonderful dreams, supplied by you and your friends, that he never wanted to wake up! It was only when you drew the line at a dream about Toffo-licious-munchy-crunchies, my dear, that he decided being awake was more interesting! It's all a question of balance, you see. Well, you must come to my talk to find out."

Fairy Buttercup is so happy that she has not hurt anyone after all that she cannot help smiling. Emmelina also feels relieved. She hates to see an unhappy fairy. As soon as the cloud arrives back in Dreamland, the two fairies are eager to tell their friends what has happened. They turn to thank the wizard one more time, but he has fallen fast asleep on the comfortable, fluffy cloud!

"Poor Wizard Moonbeam! It's been a busy day for him," says Emmelina. Suddenly a little dream bubble bursts with a *ping!* near her ear. It is a dream request from a sleepy wizard!

Emmelina can't help laughing. "I think you need to help me with this one, Buttercup!" she giggles. "You seem to know more about it than I do. Wizard Moonbeam would like a dream, please, and I don't think we should say no."

"What does he want to dream about?" asks Buttercup. Then seeing Emmelina's face, she guesses all by herself, and one clever, tired wizard is soon deep in a delicious dream about … Toffo-licious-munchy-crunchies.

A Dream for You

Dreamland fairies are busy – but they are never, ever too busy to visit *you*. When you are snuggled in your bed, or drifting off to sleep on a long journey, somewhere far away (but, as you know, very near as well) Dreamland fairies are waiting.

How do you ask for a special dream? It's easy. First you must be feeling comfortable (*not*, really *not* riding your bike or crossing the road or doing anything at all *dangerous*). Now close your eyes.

160

No! Not actually *now*! You need to be able to read this book! In a minute, when you've finished, you can close your eyes. Then you need to think about something you long to dream about. It could be anything. Start imagining how your perfect dream would begin. Remember, in dreams you can go anywhere. You can be anyone. You can do anything you want to do. Dreams are your own private world, and no Dreamland fairy will ever tell another human being what you dream about. It is an important part of the Dreamland Law.

The stories in this book take a little while to read, but fairy time is not the same as human time.

In these stories it sometimes takes a Dreamland fairy a long time to find the right dream, but years and years of fairy time are just a second to us. So before you have imagined even a minute or two of your perfect dream, the fairies will be at work, bringing you the dream you long for.

Does it always work? I think so, but sometimes it's really difficult to remember your dreams afterwards. They seem confused and strange. Trust the Dreamland fairies to bring you what you need, and remember, no one and nothing can ever harm you in a Dreamland dream. It simply wraps you safely in your own special story and carries you through to morning.

THE FAIRY

PRINCESSES

Princess
Rose's Secret

Princess Rose was a real princess, but she didn't feel like one. It was true that she lived in a palace. It was also true that her father was a king and her mother was a queen. She had three princess sisters, too. But Rose looked at her sisters and felt somehow different. They loved being princesses. They liked dancing and pretty clothes. Rose wasn't so sure. She felt happiest outside, in the shady woods and gardens around the palace.

One day Princess Rose discovered that she really *was* different, and in a most wonderful way …

It was a sunny spring morning. As usual, Princess Rose had escaped from the palace before the royal golden breakfast plates had been cleared away. She ran out into the gardens, where flowers were shyly raising their heads towards the sun, and dew drops glittered on the grass.

Princess Rose sighed with happiness. Just then, she heard a call from the palace.

"Princess Rose! Princess Rose! Time for your deportment classes! Madame Noon is here! Your sisters are waiting!"

The voice was faint. Rose could hardly hear it. The idea of spending such a beautiful day indoors, parading up and down the stairs with books on her head, filled Rose with horror. She hated deportment lessons. They were supposed to make her walk and sit and dance like a princess. But deep inside, Rose didn't want to be a princess. She just wanted to be herself.

Rose turned sadly. She didn't want to go, but she simply couldn't pretend she hadn't heard. She stood for just one more moment and closed her eyes, trying to remember the sounds and scents of the gardens.

It was then that she heard, for the very first time, a wonderful sound. It was a bird, singing nearby. The pure, high notes rolled towards her like perfect pearls. Rose felt the song swirling around her. It made her forget Madame Noon and her sisters. It made her forget she was a princess. The song was so beautiful that she could think of nothing else. As she opened her eyes, Rose saw at once a little golden bird, sitting on a branch. As he sang, it seemed as if the whole garden turned to listen.

Slowly and softly, Princess Rose walked towards the golden bird. He didn't seem afraid. In fact, it was as if his song was drawing her onwards. "Follow me, follow me," he sang. "Follow, follow, follow!" As if in a dream, Princess Rose moved silently forward. She realized that she was passing between two trees, whose trunks and twining branches made a kind of archway. And as she stepped between the trees, something amazing began to happen.

Rose suddenly felt as light as air. She saw the bright eyes of the bird and smelled the cool, mossy wood, but under her feet she felt nothing at all. And everything around her was becoming bigger and bigger.

It should have felt frightening, but somehow, Rose was happier than she had ever been. It was as if she was part of the woods and the flowers and the song of the bird. She found herself settling beside the bird, sitting on his branch in the sunlight.

It took Rose several minutes to understand what had happened to her. It was hard to believe that it was not just a dream. But sitting on the branch she slowly understood that she was now tiny, no bigger than the bird, and she could fly! You will have guessed much more quickly than she did – Rose had become a fairy!

"Don't worry," sang the bird. "You have always been a fairy princess. The time has come for you to know, that's all. It's not strange at all."

Part of Rose wanted to protest. It *was* strange! It was very strange indeed. She didn't usually eat breakfast and suddenly turn into a fairy! But another part of her knew that what the bird was saying was true. She felt just right. She was surprised and not surprised, all at the same time.

"You can talk to me!" said Rose, realizing that she had understood everything the bird had said.

The beautiful little bird put his head on one side. "Well," he sang, "I'm just singing, as I always do. It's simply that you can understand me now. In fact, you can hear what all living things are saying. Listen!"

It was true. All at once Rose understood that the wood was buzzing with little creatures. Not far away, a butterfly was talking to a friend. A beetle was showing his children their new home. And a daisy ... *oh!* ... a daisy was laughing!

Rose had never known that everything has its own voice. She was so keen to hear the little conversations that were going on all around her that she found herself floating gently from the branch and moving out into the glade.

"I'm flying!" laughed Rose. "And it's easy! Oh!" For a moment, thinking about flying made it difficult. Rose wobbled a little and felt as if she was falling.

"Smile and don't forget to breathe!" called the bird. "It really *is* easy!"

And Rose found that when she took a deep breath and smiled, she floated upright again. Soon she was flitting around the trees, enjoying a view of the woodland that she had never seen before.

Rose didn't know how long she spent there in the sunshine. She only knew that she felt happy.

The sun was high overhead when she heard
sounds from a world she had almost forgotten.

Something – no, three somethings – were
crashing through the woodland. They were
making a terrible noise.

"She must be here somewhere!" boomed
a voice nearby. "Rose! Rose!"

It was the other princesses. Their deportment
class was over, and they had come to look for
their sister.

Rose, perched on a little
branch high above them,
looked down in horror.
She didn't want to be
seen, and she didn't want
to go back. It was almost as if
the bird could read her
thoughts.

"You must go back," he said.
"It is time. You can come
again. You only have to
follow my voice and go
through the portal."

173

"Portal?" cried Rose. "I don't understand."

"It's just a doorway into your other life," explained the bird. "It can be a space between two trees. It can be a window, or a pool of water, or a shaft of sunlight. But whatever it is, you will know because I will be there. Come this way now. It's time to go."

Before she really understood what was happening, Rose found herself passing back between the trees. Suddenly, she was standing on the ground again, feeling huge and heavy, and being jostled by her sisters.

"Where have you been hiding?" they laughed. "You're in ever so much trouble at home."

It was true. Rose had to do an extra embroidery class and practise her minuet steps until it was almost dark.

"I don't understand," one of her sisters whispered to another. "She hates doing this. Why is she smiling?"

That night, Rose lay in her bed in her turret room and thought about everything that had happened. How long must she wait before she heard the golden bird again? Suddenly, she couldn't bear it any more. She wrapped her robe around herself and crept down the stairs, past the sleeping sentry and out into the garden. The moon was shining brightly. It was easy to find her way back into the woodland.

But among the trees it was darker. Everything looked different. Rose stumbled over stones and fallen branches. She couldn't find the trees where the golden bird had been. And there was something worse, she realized. The night-time sounds of the woodland were completely different, too. And there was no sound of singing.

Sadly, Rose walked back to the palace. She felt as if all the magic had gone from her life again, and she wasn't smiling any more.

Rose went back to her room.
She lay down on her bed and
closed her eyes. Shining tears
slid down her cheeks. Perhaps
it *had* been a dream, after all.

"Follow! Follow! Follow!"

From somewhere nearby, a
silvery voice trilled through the
night. Rose opened her eyes.
There, sitting in a shaft of
moonlight on the windowsill,
was the magical bird.

Rose reached the
window in a second.
As her bare foot touched
the moonlight on the floor,
she felt once more the strange, floating
feeling. She had become a fairy again!

"I'm so happy!" Rose told the bird,
standing beside him. "I thought it
had all been a dream. I came to look
for you, and you weren't there!"

"Of course not," sang the bird. "I'm not
really outside you at all. I'm inside, in your heart.

You will see me when you least expect to, but you can call me, too. If you need me, if you need to become your real self, just close your eyes and think of me. It will always work, I promise."

"I always need you!" sighed Rose. "I never want to be an ordinary princess again."

"You're not an ordinary princess," said the bird. "Surely you realize that now? You have never been an ordinary princess. You're a very special girl and you can do extraordinary things. How many girls do you know who can fly?"

Rose smiled. "No one," she whispered. "But I don't understand why this has happened to me."

"You will," promised the bird. "You will." And, as a cloud passed across the moon, and the moonlight faded, he silently disappeared.

This time, Rose didn't feel unhappy. She knew that what the bird said was true. She was smiling as she fell deeply asleep.

The next day, something happened
that made Rose forget about being a
fairy. Her mother, the Queen, was taken ill.
At first, no one was concerned. As the day passed,
however, the Queen grew worse. The King sent
for the best doctors in the land. All night, they tended
the Queen, but she grew more and more ill. Towards
morning, the oldest and wisest doctor shook his head.
"There is nothing more we can do," he told the King.

"Nothing?" cried the King. "Nothing at all? There must be
some medicine you can give her."

The doctors exchanged glances. "There was once a little
blue flower growing in this land, Sire," said one, "called the
Evening Star. Juice from its petals could cure the Queen,
but it has not been seen here for many years. Every single
flower was picked long ago."

"If we searched …," the King began, but the doctor looked grave. "It is dark," he said. "What could anyone do? Even if the plant could be found, it would be in the most distant, hidden parts of the kingdom, and I am afraid that even by the morning, it will be too late for the Queen."

When she heard this, Rose ran from the room. "If only I could do something," she sobbed. And suddenly, she knew that she could. She thought hard about the golden bird and found herself floating into the sound of his beautiful song. She didn't need to explain. "Everyone will help," he said.

Suddenly, Rose began to hear a scurrying and a whispering all around her, as hundreds and hundreds of tiny creatures told their neighbours about the Evening Star. She felt as if she was surrounded by tiny friends.

"You are," sang the bird, as if she had spoken aloud. "Now, go back to your mother."

Well before midnight, a white dove, flying slowly on silent wings, settled on the windowsill outside the Queen's room and cooed softly. Only Rose, who had been waiting and hoping, heard the sound and ran to open the window. Quickly she went over to the wise doctor and placed something in his hands. He looked up in amazement, but Rose put her finger to her lips, and he hurried away.

In all the excitement of the Queen's recovery, no one thought to ask how the Evening Star had been found, but the bird sang in Rose's heart, and she was happy.

Princess Magnolia's
Magic

When Princess Magnolia was tiny, she loved to spend the afternoons with her mother. It was very hot then, so the Queen and everyone else in the palace rested in the shade. The Queen often went to her room, where she read, or wrote letters, or slept for a while. Magnolia thought her mother was the most beautiful, wonderful woman in the world. She wanted to be just the same when she was older. So she sat quietly by the Queen and tried to do just what she did.

One afternoon, the Queen was lying on her day bed, reading, while Magnolia sat among a pile of silken cushions nearby and looked at a book, too. She couldn't read herself yet, but she loved to look at the pictures.

The Queen had some very beautiful books. Magnolia was always careful as she turned the pages. Today, Magnolia was looking at a book she had not seen before. The pictures were strange, and there were odd patterns in the margins of the pages. The little princess was enchanted by it.

Magnolia looked up as a shadow fell across her page. It was the Queen. She had an odd expression on her face.

"You've been looking at that book for a long time," she told her daughter. "Why do you like it so much?"

"I don't know," said the little girl. She grinned. "I think it's a magic book."

The Queen's eyes shone. "Magic?" she whispered. "Show me." She sat down beside Magnolia.

Gently, Magnolia turned the pages. "It's the pictures," she said. "The people in them really look at me."

"What do you mean?" Tears glittered in the Queen's eyes, but Magnolia didn't see.

"In this picture," she said, "there's a princess who smiles at me." And it was true. As the Queen looked, a girl in the picture turned her head and smiled from the page.

The Queen put her arms around her daughter.

"You are a special, special little girl," she said. "And this is our secret now. When I was young, the girl in the picture smiled at me, too. That was how I knew that I was not just an ordinary princess. I was a fairy princess. And now I can see that you are a fairy princess, too. When you are older, you will be able to do amazing things."

"We can do them together," said Magnolia. She loved her mother so much, she wasn't a bit surprised to find that she could do magic.

But the Queen sighed. "No," she said. "I am not a fairy princess any more. I am a queen now. I don't have magic powers any longer."

"*I* think you're magic!" said Magnolia, hugging her mother.

Time passed, and Magnolia grew prettier every day. But she still couldn't do magic, and she began to think that she wasn't a fairy princess after all. Her mother found her one day staring at her schoolbooks. Magnolia slammed a book down in disgust. "I'm not

magic at all," she pouted. "I've been trying to say a spell to do my sums for me. It didn't work!"

"I'm not surprised," said the Queen. "Didn't you know that you can only do magic if it helps someone else? You can never do magic to help yourself."

"But when will I learn?"

"You won't start doing magic when *you* want to," her mother replied. "The magic has to come to you. It happens in a special way, but I can't help. It will happen when it happens."

A few weeks later, the Queen and King had to go away on a royal visit. Magnolia stayed at home. There were servants to look after her, but she still felt a little lonely and sad.

One evening, as Magnolia sat alone in her room, she heard a beautiful sound. It was a bird, singing his heart out. Magnolia ran to the window, but there was no sign of a bird in the golden light of evening. Besides, the sound seemed to be coming from inside the room. Magnolia turned. Something strange was happening … at last! On the walls of the room were painted flowers and birds and twirling vines. One golden bird was singing!

Magnolia hardly had time to feel excited. She walked towards the bird. The song began to swirl around her. It was as if the music was sweeping her up. She couldn't feel the floor beneath her feet. She was flying! "It's magic!" cried Magnolia, joyfully.

"Now you are a fairy princess," sang the bird, "the whole world will be magic for you."

Magnolia looked around. She was whirling across the room, and all around her wonderful things were happening. Flowers were blooming on the walls. Stars were shimmering all around. Magnolia swept her hand through the air, and rose petals fell from her fingertips.

"This is your magic," sang the bird. "You can make things beautiful wherever you go. Wherever you find me, I will lead you into your very own magical world."

In the morning, Princess Magnolia woke on a pile of satin cushions and wondered if it had all been a dream. But when she looked around, the walls were still covered with beautiful flowers, and there were rose petals on the floor.

Magnolia stood up. She felt heavy and awkward. She couldn't fly, and when she waved her hand, nothing magical happened at all. Then she remembered that she must find the bird to help her. But strangely, all the birds on the walls had their heads turned.

Magnolia listened as hard as she could, but there was no singing to be heard. She felt very sorry for herself.

Magnolia spent the next few weeks in a kind of daze. She was so unsure about what had happened that she didn't even tell her mother about it. She could think of nothing but her own disappointment.

The Queen could tell that something was wrong, but the flowers had faded from the walls. She did not know what had happened to her daughter.

"Next time we have to go away," she told her husband, "we must take Magnolia, too. It isn't good for a young girl to be left alone."

So it happened that a month or so later, the royal party set off to visit the farthest region of the kingdom. Magnolia was quiet and sad, as she had been since the summer. All went well, until one night, when rain lashed down and wild winds blew, the royal party was forced to shelter in a town at the foot of the mountains.

The next morning, the day dawned grey but fine. Magnolia stepped out into the watery light and was shocked by what she saw. The town was pitiful. Buildings were broken and battered. A dust filled the streets, the gardens and even the houses. Worse than that, the people themselves looked dull and defeated. They seemed to have lost all hope and were simply dragging themselves from day to day.

When Magnolia's parents appeared, a local man explained that a volcano had erupted a year before, covering everything in its deadly ash. Now nothing would grow, and the town itself was dying.

Magnolia felt as though her heart would break. Suddenly, she had no thought for herself at all. Behind her, she could hear her parents hurrying away to discuss with their officials what could be done to help these people, but they were talking of weeks and months and years.

Then Magnolia noticed a little bird, scratching in the dust. And as she watched, it turned towards her. Surely, beneath the dust, it was a golden bird? Magnolia reached out her hand, very gently and carefully. The bird bent its head for a moment, and then it sang!

Magnolia felt herself whirling in the swirl of sound. She stretched out her arms, and suddenly, wonderful things began to happen. From the dust, flowers began to bloom. Grey faces lifted and smiled. And all the birds in the town began to sing.

Magnolia smiled, too. At last she understood what being a fairy princess was all about.

Princess
Daisy's
Darkness

There was once a princess who was afraid of the dark. She didn't know why she was afraid, but at night she insisted that the lamp beside her bed should be kept burning. It didn't help that Princess Daisy lived in a northern country, where summer days were light until very late, but winter days were almost as dark as night. Daisy dreaded the winters and longed for the summer light. Then, when summer came, she could not enjoy it because she knew that winter would come again.

It was during the summer that Princess Daisy first discovered she was a fairy princess. She was walking through the pinewoods with her dog on a bright, sunny day. The trees were shady, but here and there, golden pools of sunlight shimmered on the path. Daisy and Tor, the dog, played a game, chasing each other from one patch of sunlight to the next. At last, laughing but out of breath, Daisy threw herself down to rest under a tree. Tor flopped down beside her.

At first, all they could hear was their own breathing. Then, quite suddenly, a bird began to sing nearby. It was the most beautiful sound that Daisy had ever heard.

Daisy looked around. She spotted the singer sitting on a branch in a shaft of sunlight. He seemed to glow gold in the light. Daisy had never seen such a bird before.

Then Princess Daisy noticed something very strange. Tor was trotting away through the trees. Usually, he never left her side. Daisy always felt safe with Tor. Now he was leaving, yet she didn't feel frightened at all. In fact, the song of the bird seemed to be filling her with a golden happiness. Daisy was not at all surprised when she rose lightly into the air and above the trees, out into the sunlight above.

Daisy could see the forest stretching away. She could see the mountains in the distance. Above the trees, the turrets of her castle home sparkled and shone. "The bird will look after me," Daisy thought.

"No-o," the bird's song floated up. "You'll look after yourself!"

It was true! Daisy found that she only had to concentrate a little bit to fly wherever she wanted. High in the bright air, she didn't ever want to go back amongst the trees.

Suddenly, from far below, Daisy heard a dreadful howling sound. It was Tor! Daisy could tell at once that he was frightened and in pain, and soon she knew why. It was as though the handsome dog was speaking to her.

"He's caught in a trap!" gasped Daisy, and she flew down towards the sound. It was only when she flew past the first branches of the trees that Daisy realized something she had not noticed before. She was tiny! Somehow, when the bird sang, she had become much smaller.

But Daisy didn't have time to think about her size. Tor's howls were becoming fainter. At last, the princess fluttered down beside her dog. His paw was caught in a vicious, metal trap. His head was lying on the mossy ground, and his eyes were closed.

Daisy went at once to open the trap, but it would have been impossible even at her normal size. Now there was nothing she could do. Tears ran down Daisy's face. Tor was going to die, and she could not help.

"You can do it! Magic is all you need!" sang the bird. Daisy lifted her head. Whatever could it mean? She didn't know how to do magic. She felt hopeless.

The bird was singing again. "You didn't know how to fly, either. How did you do that?"

Daisy thought quickly. "I don't know," she whispered. "And I don't know how to do this either, but I will try."

She closed her eyes and imagined Tor running free across a hillside. *Snap!* The iron hinges fell apart, but Tor lay still. Daisy knew that she could not lift him, but somehow she had to get help. Again, she closed her eyes.

She imagined men running through the forest, looking for her and the dog. Almost as soon as the picture had flashed through her head, she heard a thundering of feet and shouts as her father's woodmen ran into the clearing.

In a flash, Daisy fluttered into the trees. She didn't know how she could explain that she had changed. She needn't have worried. As the men bent over the dog, Daisy felt a heaviness and found herself sinking to the ground. She was her real size again.

It took a long time for Tor to recover from his wounds. Daisy looked after him every day. At night, he slept by her bed. She was so busy thinking about Tor that she hardly noticed summer passing. Of course, from time to time she wondered about the extraordinary things that had happened to her. She began to think it had all been a dream.

Then, one evening, there was a coolness in the air, and Daisy noticed that it was getting dark. She felt a great sadness well up inside her. That night she whispered to Tor, "You love the summer as much as I do. I wish the winter would not come for us."

Suddenly, outside the window, she heard a bird singing. Then another, and another. She threw open her heavy curtains. It was no longer dark outside! The summer had returned!

Princess Daisy slept well that night, with her windows open to the garden and the soft light of a summer night falling on her pillow. In the morning, she put on a cotton dress and ran happily down to breakfast.

She realized at once that no one else felt the same. Her parents frowned and looked worried.

"It's not right," said her mother. "Something dreadful is going to happen. I know it!"

"I will summon my wisest advisers," replied the King. "They will know why this has happened."

The servants scuttled about their business, not daring to look up. They were frightened. They didn't understand why winter had suddenly turned into summer.

There were other problems, too. In the forests, animals were found, ill and distressed, beside the paths. Great bears and tiny mice, who usually spent the winter asleep in caves and among tree roots, had been woken by the light. They did not know what to do.

In the gardens, trees turned yellow and branches drooped.

"Poor things, they need their winter's rest," said the Queen. "I'm afraid we shall lose many of them."

Princess Daisy felt guilty and sad. She knew in her heart that it was her magic that had changed winter to summer. Although she loved the sunshine so much, she knew what she must do.

Princess Daisy tried wishing, but nothing happened. Why had she been able to wish for winter to end but now could not make it return? There was only one thing to do. She must find the bird and ask his advice.

Daisy wandered into the woods and listened for the song that had filled her with happiness all those months before. She heard nothing. Even the ordinary birdsong sounded somehow wrong. Daisy ran back to the castle and called for Tor.

"You can find the bird, Tor," she whispered, stroking his rough coat. The faithful dog put his head on one side and set off towards the forest. He led Daisy further than she had ever been before.

It was gloomy among the trees. The princess felt uneasy. Then, suddenly, she heard the song she had longed for.

The golden bird was singing as if its heart would break. Daisy burst into tears. "I'm sorry," she whispered.

"I'm sorry, too," sang the bird. "Do not be afraid of the darkness, dear child. We need these quiet times, just as we need to sleep and rest."

"I know that now," said Daisy quietly. "I will never use magic again if you can put this right."

"You were born to use magic," the bird seemed to say. "You just need to learn how to use it properly. I can teach you. Now, you can help me to bring back the winter, but we will do it slowly, so that the plants and animals are not afraid."

So it was that the days grew colder, and the nights grew darker, and everything was back as it should be. Daisy had learned to love the darkness and to use her magic wisely, and the kingdom was happy once more.

The Princesses'
Presents

All families are magical in their own way, but some families are more magical than others. King Constant had seven daughters, and *all* of them were fairy princesses. This sometimes made life very difficult for the King, who had no idea at all how to do magic himself.

The eldest princess was called Aurelia. She was seventeen at the time of this story. Her sisters were Bella (fifteen), Claudia (thirteen), Delia (eleven), Eugenia (nine), Fiona (seven), and Giggles (five). Giggles' real name was Georgina, but no one ever called her that.

The princesses had a problem. It wasn't a horrible problem, but it was a problem all the same. King Constant had a Very Big Birthday in a month's time. The princesses wanted to give him a Really Special Present, but they couldn't decide what it should be.

"I think he'd like a dolls' house," said Giggles. "A really big one, looking like our palace, with little dolls inside looking like us!"

The older girls frowned. "That's not what *he* would like," they said. "That's what *you* would like!" Giggles had to admit this was true, though she still thought it was a good present for anyone!

"I think he'd like a horse," suggested Bella. "A white stallion from the hills. They would look wonderful at parades."

"Father likes his old horse," said Aurelia. "A stallion from the hills might be, well, livelier than he could manage at his age."

The girls agreed. They thought the King was about to be Very Old Indeed.

"I know what he would really like," said Fiona quietly. "He'd like a holiday. A real holiday without any parades, or people shaking his hand, or trumpets, or banquets. He'd like to wear old clothes and not have to think about being the King."

All the princesses turned to look at Fiona. This really was a very good idea. Their father often looked tired, and official holidays always involved lots of parades, and people shaking his hand, and trumpets, and banquets. A proper holiday was just what he needed for his Very Big Birthday.

"Well, there's only one thing to decide," said Aurelia. "Where should we send him?"

"Tahiti!" cried Bella. "He'd love the sunshine."

"Switzerland!" shouted Claudia. "He's always wanted to learn to ski."

"Brazil!" yelled Delia. "He could paddle down the Amazon and have adventures."

"Australia!" Eugenia was sure she had the answer. "He could go surfing. No one would recognize him in shorts!"

"China!" Fiona had seen pictures of the Great Wall. She knew her father would love to say he had walked along it.

Giggles hadn't studied as much geography as her sisters. "The Moon!" she screeched, to drown out the others. "In a rocket!"

Aurelia, as the eldest, felt it was her job to make a decision. It was difficult. "I think he'd love all those places," she said slowly. "And Egypt, which was my idea. Do you think we should ask him where he would really like to go?"

"NO!" chorused the other girls. "It has to be a surprise. It's not a Really Special Present if he knows about it."

Aurelia admitted that this was true. "Maybe we could find out without exactly asking," she said. "We could be clever about it. That means you keep quiet, Giggles!"

The King was busy all that day, and it was late when he came home. The princesses decided that breakfast the next morning might be the best time to try to find out where he would really like to go.

One by one, the princesses went to bed. The King, tired from saluting and shaking hands, retired to his royal bedchamber as well. Quietness reigned in the palace, and in the empty corridors, only a few lanterns glimmered.

But no one was having a peaceful night! In their rooms, the princesses tossed and turned. Princess Aurelia wished she had tried harder to persuade her sisters that Egypt was the best place. She could so vividly imagine the King strolling under palm trees beside the River Nile, or swaying along on a camel with the Pyramids in the distance.

Bella and Claudia shared a room. They were whispering together in the darkness. "I think you might be right about Switzerland," hissed Bella. "I've always wanted to learn to ski, too. Perhaps we could go with him. Anyway, can't you imagine the King whizzing down a mountain? He'd love it!"

"I know," whispered Claudia sharply. "That's why I suggested it!"

Both girls lay awake, gazing into the darkness, imagining the fun their father (and his daughters) would have in the Alps.

Delia and Eugenia shared, too, but they could not agree. "There are huge snakes in the Amazon," Delia enthused.

"Well, he wouldn't like *that*!" growled Eugenia. "They're dangerous!"

"There are sharks and poisonous spiders in Australia," Delia reminded her. "What makes you think he'd want to see *them*?"

Eugenia suddenly had a vision of her father being pursued by a great white shark. She brushed the thought away. "A shark wouldn't dare to try to eat a king," she said, hoping this was true.

In their room, Fiona and Giggles were not at all worried by little details like geography and the frontiers of science. "He could go to China first," said Fiona, "then fly from there to the Moon. We could look out at night and wave to him. He could be King of the Moon!"

"And we could be Moon Princesses," said Giggles. "That would be lovely. I can just imagine my shiny moony dress."

Awake in their beds, all the princesses were imagining. Poor King Constant! You see, when fairy princesses think hard enough about something, especially something that is good for someone else, it very often happens. While the princesses thought and dreamed, the King was hurtling around the world, in the snow one minute and the ocean the next. He'd just got used to strolling beside the Nile when he was whisked off to the Moon! No sooner had he begun to feel comfortable there than he found himself nose to fang with a deadly snake! It was dreadful! And all in his best royal pyjamas!

Knowing nothing of this, the princesses arrived at breakfast the next morning, determined to find out where their father would most like to be taken on holiday.

"Dearest Papa," Aurelia began, "you are looking tired. Wouldn't you like a little holiday?"

Then she rubbed her eyes and looked again. Her father really *was* looking tired. In fact, it was as if he hadn't slept in weeks!

"Are you quite well, Papa?" she asked.

"No, I'm not!" cried the King. "I feel as though I've been dragged around the world all night long. I never want to see a foreign country again! Or the Moon!"

The princesses exchanged guilty glances. They guessed what had happened. They were disappointed, too. Giggles, who had not yet learnt to be tactful, blurted out what they had all been thinking. "But now we can't send you on holiday for your birthday!"

The King looked around at seven sad faces. Although he didn't really understand about magic or what had happened, he hated to see his daughters so unhappy.

"Well, there is one thing I would really love for my birthday," he said, "and that is to have my portrait painted with the most beautiful princesses in the world. Yes, I mean *you*!"

Well, Giggles found it hard to keep still, and Bella would keep talking, but no one met a poisonous snake or a shark, and everyone was happy with the result.

Princess Nerina's
Problem

Princess Nerina discovered that she was a fairy princess when she was very small. She loved it! Although she knew that she should use her magical powers to help people, she soon realized that she could have a lot of fun as well. One morning, as she watched her father put on his kingly robes, she began to wonder what they would look like if they were more interesting than the usual royal red. No sooner had the idea drifted into her head than the robes became quite extraordinary!

Nerina concentrated hard and put things right straight away. The King decided he had been imagining things and must get more sleep.

After that, Nerina had a lot of fun decorating her bedroom. It was brilliant! Not only was it the most gorgeous room in the house, but when she heard her mother coming down the corridor, she could quickly magic it back to pink and purple.

As she grew older, Nerina grew bolder! One day, walking in the gardens, she suddenly decided to change all the domes on the palace. Usually a simple pale green shade, they looked wonderful in purple, gold, orange and pink. A passing pigeon fluttered down in shock. The princess sighed happily, until she heard her mother's voice. "Nerina! Change those domes back at once! What would your father think?"

Nerina jumped. She thought she had been alone. The Queen was marching across the lawn. She certainly did not look happy.

"Now look here, Nerina," she said, "I know you love to do magic. I did, too, at your age. But you must be more discreet. Not everyone is happy about this kind of thing. Your father would prefer to believe that magic doesn't exist. It worries him. Now please be more careful in future."

Nerina promised. She sometimes changed the flowers in the ballroom from white to pink (when no one was there, of course). She once sat at a very, very boring banquet and amused herself by changing her underwear from green to orange to purple to red all through dinner without anyone knowing at all!

Princesses are not often alone. They are usually surrounded by courtiers and servants, or waving to crowds of people. But everyone needs to be alone sometimes, so Nerina loved to ride out on her horse Palmira. At first her father insisted that soldiers and servants went with her, but after a while his daughter persuaded him to let her ride across the wide, open grasslands by herself.

It was on these rides that Princess Nerina got into the bad habit of having fun with her magic when she thought no one could see. Palmira was a beautiful white horse, but when she was out of sight of the palace, Nerina changed her to a gleaming jet black. Palmira seemed to like it. She tossed her head and galloped faster.

This gave Nerina an idea. She changed her own long, blonde hair to jet black, too. The girl and her horse looked very striking, riding like the wind across the bending grasses, hair and mane and tail streaming out behind them.

That was the sight that caught the eye of Prince Averne, riding home himself from a visit to his grandmother. The moment that he saw the amazing girl on her wonderful horse, he decided that he must marry her. She was unlike anyone he had ever seen.

Nerina, speeding by, didn't even notice the young man, but Averne had seen the coronet on her saddlecloth. That night he presented himself at the royal palace.

The King greeted him, as one royal person should greet another, and asked how he could help his visitor. Prince Averne came straight to the point. "I would like to marry your daughter," he said.

"I confess that I saw her today as she rode across the plain, and I do not think that I can live without her. My family is a good one, as you know, and I will inherit my parents' kingdom one day. You can ask anyone about me. I feel sure that I would be a good husband for her, and you can be sure that I would always love and care for her."

The King was startled. It was true that Nerina was now old enough to be married, but it hadn't occurred to him that the event would happen so soon. The young man seemed ideal, but there were other things to consider. One thing in particular.

The King cleared his throat. "For what it is worth," he said, "I should be delighted to welcome you as a son-in-law, but this is not a decision for me to make. The princess must say herself whom she will marry. However, I see no harm in introducing you."

The King hurried off to tell his wife what had happened. Together, they rushed to Nerina's room. On the way, they agreed that too many details might put her off. "Just a casual meeting," said the King. "Who knows, she might be as smitten by him as he obviously is by her."

When the Queen had finished fussing over Nerina's hair, the royal family arrived back in the receiving room. The prince looked up eagerly.

"May I present my daughter, the Princess Nerina," the King announced. Nerina, seeing a most handsome young man before her, made her very best curtsey. She certainly did like what she saw.

But the prince took a step backwards. "I'm sorry," he said, "but there has been some misunderstanding. Oh dear, this is embarrassing. It is your other daughter I mean. The one with raven hair who rides a magnificent black horse."

The King and Queen looked at each other in puzzlement. Nerina gulped and tried to look innocent, while furiously thinking about what to do. While the King and Queen explained that she was their only daughter, and the prince apologized for troubling them as politely as he could, Princess Nerina was able to look at him more carefully and listen to him talking. He was desperately handsome, funny and clever, she decided. What could she do?

Bowing low, the prince backed out of the room. "I'll show him out," gasped Nerina, and before her parents could speak, she had seized the prince's arm and dragged him into the corridor.

I simply cannot let him go, thought Nerina. I will simply have to tell him the truth. He is young. Surely he can't be bothered about magic? As quickly as she could, Nerina explained that it had been she with raven hair and a magnificent black horse.

Prince Averne looked thunderstruck. Was the girl mad? "Don't they have magic in your country?" cried Nerina. The prince shook his head, backing away again.

Princess Nerina decided that desperate circumstances needed desperate deeds. She pulled the prince under a chandelier and in an instant changed herself into the girl he had seen that morning. The poor prince almost fainted, the shock was so great.

"Or you might prefer this!" cried Nerina desperately. In an instant she had orange hair, blue hair and purple hair. In her panic, she didn't concentrate and gave herself a green face as well. It wasn't an attractive look. The prince's face became more and more concerned. With a strangled cry, he turned and ran.

Poor Nerina fled to her bedroom and refused to come out for three days. The more she thought about Prince Averne, the surer she became that she wanted to spend her life with him. But it was dreadful that he was disgusted by her magical powers.

In desperation, Nerina went to her mother. "I don't want to be a fairy princess any more," she said. "There must be something I can do to give up my powers."

The Queen smiled. "I imagine that this has something to do with a certain prince," she said. "You know, there is nothing to worry about. When you are married, your magic will disappear quite naturally, just as mine did when I married your father. It has always been that way. Your only problem, my girl, is finding a way to let Prince Averne know that."

In the end, there was no problem. Prince Averne, too, had shut himself in his room for days. When his mother asked what was wrong, the story came tumbling out.

"I like the sound of your Princess Nerina," said the Queen. Then she told him just what Nerina's mother had told her. "I was a fairy princess myself once," she said. "So I know."

So it was that Prince Averne once more rode out towards the palace of the girl he loved. At this meeting, Nerina controlled herself. As a matter of fact, she was so busy staring into her prince's blue eyes that she didn't even think about doing magic. Two days later, both kingdoms were rejoicing at the news of the royal engagement, and fairy princesses from far and wide looked forward to the wedding.

Many Kinds of Magic

Most invitations to the wedding of Princess Nerina and Prince Averne were sent by messenger or mail. They were written in gold on thick, cream card, with the crests of both families at the top. Royal families far and near eagerly waited for their arrival. Some special invitations, however, were not sent but sung. A certain golden bird made sure that fairy princesses everywhere knew of the wedding long before anyone else.

So it was that two days before the wedding, all the rooms of Princess Nerina's palace and several of the grander houses nearby were filled with royal guests and the many servants they felt they needed to bring.

All seemed set for a wonderful wedding day until the King's Weather Watcher, a very old man with a long, white beard, asked to see His Majesty.

"Well, really," cried the King, who was having final adjustments made to his royal robes, "I'm much too busy to see him now. Tell him to come back on Thursday."

But the old man sent back a message at once to say that Thursday would be too late. Much, much too late.

"Very well," sighed the King. "Send him in. But he only has two minutes. I need to consult with the royal cooks again."

The Weather Watcher shuffled into the room. "Sire," he said, "I fear that I have bad news."

It seemed that a blizzard of huge proportions was heading towards the palace from the mountains far away across the plains.

The King went pale. Then he strode quickly around the room, looking out of each of the many windows of the tower room. In every direction, the sky was blue and sunny.

The King didn't wish to be unkind. "My dear old fellow, you have worked hard for me for more years than I can remember. Perhaps it is time you retired," he said. "After the wedding we can have a little party for you. How about it?"

The old man tried to protest, but the King had too much on his mind to worry about something as unlikely as a blizzard.

227

He sent the Weather Watcher away and thought no more about snow … until he woke up the next morning.

For that night, when everyone was asleep – even the boy who kept the lanterns alight in the palace courtyards – more visitors came to the palace. They were little white, whirling visitors, swirling thick and fast from the inky sky. In an hour, the gardens and roofs were covered with a crisp, white layer that sparkled in the moonlight. In two hours, doorways were blocked and paths filled knee-deep with snow. By the time the lantern-boy awoke, and the cockerels were stirring on the royal farm, the whole kingdom was unrecognizable.

As far as the eye could see, the world was white. It looked beautiful, but it was, for a king planning a wedding, disastrous. On the day that should have been one of the happiest of his life, the King sat with his head in his hands, too anxious even to pace up and down.

Every road in the kingdom was blocked. Nothing and no one could reach the palace. And on the day of the royal wedding, there was a very great deal that needed to reach the palace.

The Queen, trying to be practical, made a list of everything that was lacking for the ceremony. It didn't make her or her husband feel any better.

most of the food
most of the wine
flowers for the cathedral
trimmings for Nerina's dress
musicians
white horses for carriages
open roads for carriages
and last but not least …
Prince Averne!

"Where is he exactly?" groaned the King, referring to his future son-in-law.

"Only two miles away, but it might as well be two hundred," replied the Queen. "We could manage, perhaps, without the other things, but you cannot have a wedding without a groom!"

Princess Nerina was even more upset. She sat in her room in despair, using her magic to turn everything she owned black or purple or a hideous shade of green to suit her mood. In a much smaller room opposite, another princess watched with interest as the curtains she could see from her window changed to green. It was Princess Rose, who had travelled to the palace with her sisters and parents a few days earlier.

She realized at once that the snow would cause big problems for the expected wedding.

I wish I could help, she thought, but my magic is not great enough to solve all the trouble this snow has brought. Just then, she heard a familiar sound. A golden voice was singing from just outside the window. At once, Rose understood what the bird was telling her.

"There are more of us!" she gasped. "Of course! Why didn't I realize that? If Nerina is a fairy princess and I am one, there must be others, too. And some of them are here!"

At the very same moment, in another part of the castle, the seven fairy daughters of King Constant had realized the same thing. As you will remember, when those girls think about something, it tends to happen. In an instant, their room was full of princesses – very special ones! All of them had been brought there by the power of the girls' magical thoughts.

"What's happening?" Nerina was not pleased. She looked in astonishment at the other princesses. Most of them she had never met before.

Princess Rose was there, of course. She quickly realized what had happened and looked around with interest at the other girls. The seven princess sisters smiled as they were joined by Princesses Magnolia and Daisy, too. As the eldest visitor, Princess Aurelia decided it was up to her to take charge. She clapped her hands.

"Your Royal Highnesses," she began. "I think I understand what is happening here. Like you, my sisters and I are fairy princesses. I think we can all guess that we are here to help Princess Nerina on her special day. Let's introduce ourselves to each other for a few moments and then settle down to work out what we can do."

There was a buzz of excitement in the room. Eleven fairy princesses hurried around the room, greeting each other. Little Princess Georgina (usually known as Giggles) felt that there were more important things to be done. She shut her eyes hard and imagined drinks and cookies, which magically appeared at a long table at one end of the room.

"Well done, Giggles," whispered Aurelia, as the princesses all began to gather around the table.

As the princesses took their places, everyone turned to Aurelia once more, but she shook her head. "This is Princess Nerina's palace," she said, "and it is her special day. She should be in charge."

It was Nerina's turn to smile. "Not at all," she said. "I am so nervous and worried that I can't think straight." The fact that the plate of cookies in front of her immediately turned a ghastly shade of green proved this!

Princess Aurelia nodded gravely. "Then I will speak," she said, "but I would like everyone else to add their own ideas."

Aurelia took a sip of her drink. "Now," she said, "the first thing we need to do is to find out exactly what the biggest problems are."

"I can help you there," sighed Nerina. "My mother has made a list. Look!" And she showed the other princesses what her mother had written.

"We'll start at the beginning," said Aurelia. "It seems that a lot of food is stuck in villages nearby but has not yet reached the palace. What can we do about that?"

For the first time, Princess Nerina looked a little less anxious. "Well, the smallest princess here has already shown how good she is at magicking a feast," she said. "Perhaps she could help?"

Giggles looked ready to burst with pride, but she was worried that preparing a huge wedding banquet might not be quite as easy as conjuring up some drinks and cookies. Her sisters Bella, Claudia, Delia and Eugenia came to stand beside her. "We will help Giggles," they said. "If the royal chef could give us the menu for this evening, we will see what we can do."

"That is easily arranged," Nerina promised.

"Now," Aurelia glanced at the list, "we seem to have no wine, either. Giggles is much too young to have anything to do with that."

Princess Nerina was looking happier every moment. "I can help with that, too," she said. "There is plenty of wine in the palace cellars, but it is of the very best kind. My father was not planning to serve it to the hundreds of guests here today. But if I tell him he must do it for the wedding of his only daughter, then I am sure he will. Cross that off your list, too, Aurelia!"

Aurelia smiled. "We are doing well," she commented, "but the next two items are more difficult. We need flowers for the cathedral, which is luckily nearby, and trimmings for Nerina's dress. They were to have been flowers, too."

"My dress could be plain," sighed Nerina. "It is not the most important thing in the world."

"But it is!" Little Princess Magnolia spoke for the first time. "You must look beautiful on your wedding day. I can see that there are no flowers to be found around the palace, now that the snow has come, but I think I can help. I will dance for you."

"My dear, you are very kind, but how will that help?" asked Nerina.

Magnolia simply said, "Watch!"

She got up from her seat and gracefully twirled across the room. As she went, the carpet bloomed with roses, and rose petals began to fall like snowflakes from the ceiling.

The other princesses clapped their hands delightedly. "This is going to be the most beautiful wedding there has ever been!" cried Nerina, with tears in her eyes.

Aurelia's eyes were back on the list. "The musicians are not yet here," she said gravely. "A wedding without music would be a sad event."

The princesses sat in silence. Suddenly a pure, golden song came from the windowsill. It was the magical bird, and at the sound of his voice, Princess Rose looked up and laughed.

"Of course!" she exclaimed. "I am able to understand all the tiny creatures of the world, and to speak to them, too. I will summon all the birds in the kingdom. The snow will not stop them from flying to us. You will have the loveliest music on earth, Nerina."

Aurelia was feeling more confident as she read the next two items on the list. "The white horses, which come, I believe from the plains far away," she said, "are not yet here. And even if they *were* here, the roads are impassable. Although the cathedral is nearby, a princess cannot walk to her wedding. How are the royal carriages to get through the streets?"

"I can help with that," said Princess Daisy. "My magic enables me to change the seasons. I learned my lesson once when I tried to stop the winter from coming. Everything went wrong, and no one was truly happy. I would not like to try to magic away all the snow, but I think I could clear it away from the courtyards and the road to the cathedral. In fact, I have an idea of what we might do with all the snow that would need to be moved."

"That still leaves us with the problem of the white horses," said Aurelia.

"There are plenty of carriage horses in the royal stables," Nerina replied, "and I can make them white in an instant. That is not at all difficult. Now, Aurelia, aren't you forgetting the most important problem of all?"

"Not at all!" Aurelia was grinning now. "My sisters and I can transport many people a short distance, which is how you all come to be here now, but we can also transport one person a long distance. Just ask my father! I myself will make sure that Prince Averne is here in time. Now, my dears, there is so much to do. Let us be busy. In five hours' time, Princess Nerina is to be married!"

The King was amazed to see his daughter, who an hour before had looked unhappier than he had ever seen her, smiling as she ran along the corridor towards her room.

"Why aren't you getting ready, Father?" she called. "Don't you know I'm getting married today? It's going to be the most wonderful wedding ever!"

It was true. No one who was there could ever forget the wedding of Prince Averne and Princess Nerina. In the banqueting hall, an amazing feast awaited the guests. The road to the cathedral still had a light covering of snow, but the carriages passed over it with ease. And along the route, beautiful columns and arches had been built with the snow that had been cleared away.

Nerina's carriage was pulled by perfect white horses, and her dress, when she stood on the steps of the cathedral to wave to the people, was wonderfully decorated with flowers of white and the palest pink. Drops of dew sparkled like diamonds among the petals.

In fact, there were flowers everywhere. Magnolia had danced as she had never danced before. The cathedral was full of beautiful blooms, while festoons of blossoms were draped over buildings and carriages.

Among the flowers, tiny songbirds filled the air with the most beautiful music.

Everyone was amazed by the magnificence of the event, but Prince Averne was the most surprised of all. One moment he was sitting sadly by his window, watching the hands of the stable clock tick slowly towards the hour when he should be by his bride's side. The next moment, he was standing in the cathedral, watching the most beautiful girl in the world float down the aisle towards him.

Of course, the fairy princesses were bridesmaids, and as they followed Princess Nerina and her husband out into the sunshine, their hearts sang with the birds fluttering overhead. The crowd outside burst into applause.

It was then that Giggles, looking down at the carriage awaiting the newly married couple, gasped, "Oh no! Nerina has forgotten to make the horses white again!"

Princess Aurelia bent down. "She hasn't forgotten, sweetheart," she said. "It's just that now that she is married, she cannot be a fairy princess like us any more, and she cannot do magic."

"Oh, that is so sad!" cried Giggles. "Poor Nerina!"

But Nerina, who was gazing up at her new husband with sparkling eyes, heard the little girl's cry. Still smiling up at her prince, she said softly, "No, it's not sad. This is another kind of magic."